MY
LITTLE
GEORGIE

MY LITTLE GEORGIE

David Warren Swartley

Cover Illustration by Brenda Mann

BETHEL
Publishing

Dedicated with affection to
Wayne, Charlie, Jon, and Kevin

MY
LITTLE
GEORGIE

Chapter 1

Greg Larwell's life would not be the same after opening the door to his fourteen-by-seventy mobile home that cold and windy March afternoon. Working out of his own home as a free-lance designer had many advantages, freedom and independence to mention two.

Greg had some understanding of the significance of that door's opening, of the magnitude of all it would involve. It not only meant opening the door literally, but opening the door of his life to someone else—a small boy rejected by his mother and relatives.

Having the distinction of being one of two single, male foster parents in the county was an honor. It had been seven long months since he first applied. During that time the county's Department of Public Welfare had not responded except to tell him he was accepted and was licensed by the state. On paper it had seemed like a good thing to do. But was he ready? Sometime during his twenty-six years of life had he become self-centered . . . maybe even selfish? Could he consider another person's needs and wants enough for *him* to give and love?

Six-year-old Georgie Stainer stepped inside the doorway. His straggly blond hair was dirty and windblown. With one hand he clutched a paper bag containing all the material possessions he owned in the world—a paper bag containing two pairs of jeans, two shirts, and one broken toy fire truck. No underwear, no socks, no toothbrush . . . nothing more.

The sudden reality of Georgie Stainer's presence struck Greg. Many things flashed through his mind. Janet Huntley would leave and the little boy would stay. Miss Huntley and Greg had talked about foster parenting, and now the time was here. Greg tried to smile warmly and to look at ease.

"Hello, Greg. How are you?" Miss Huntley smiled and gestured toward Georgie. "I have someone I'd like for you to meet."

Georgie's wide sky blue eyes cased his new home. He loosened Miss Huntley's hand from his and set the paper bag on the floor. It was obvious to Greg that Georgie was nervous and scared, as Georgie quickly grabbed Miss Huntley's hand again. His limbs were tensed as in robot style. Georgie mechanically tilted his head up toward Greg. His eyes widened more and filled with tears. Greg felt himself being sized up by this little person. Georgie's lips pursed and his eyebrows narrowed. His jaw quivered and quickly he buried his head in Miss Huntley's coat.

Miss Huntley stroked Georgie's hair for a few seconds, saying repeatedly, "That's okay, Georgie. It'll be all right." Greg reached out and patted Georgie's shoulder. Soon the crying subsided and Georgie wiped his eyes on his coat sleeve. Miss Huntley turned Georgie to face Greg and quietly cleared her throat. "Georgie, this is Greg Larwell. Greg Larwell, Georgie Stainer." Tense smiles were exchanged between Greg and Georgie.

Miss Huntley continued, "Greg, do you want Georgie to call you Greg, or Mr. Larwell, or—"

"Oh, Greg is fine," Greg nervously interrupted. "Here, let me take your coat, Georgie." Greg helped take off his coat, and Georgie meekly stepped into the living room and sat on the floor in front of the television set.

Georgie looked up at Greg and Miss Huntley and smiled faintly. "You can call me Georgie," he said in a high-pitched, squeaky voice. Then he broke into an ear-to-ear grin and everyone chuckled.

"Is this thing color?" Georgie pointed his index finger toward the TV's dial. "I like color TV's."

"No, sorry," smiled Greg. "It's just plain old black and white."

"Oh, well. That's okay," Georgie said apologetically. He looked embarrassed for asking. "I like black and whites, too." Georgie turned on **ON** button and spelled out loud, "O-N. On. That spells **on**!" He smiled proudly as if he had just unveiled a top-secret disclosure.

"I think cartoons are on. Do you want to watch cartoons, Georgie?"

"Yeah!" Georgie cheered and clapped his hands. "I love cartoons. Is Popeye on now?"

Greg looked in the *TV Guide.* "No. But Mickey Mouse is. Is that okay?"

"Sure." Georgie settled on the carpet, lying on his stomach with chin in hands. If a stranger had walked in, he would have assumed Georgie had lived there for a long time.

Greg reached for the dial to change to the correct channel. "Hey!" Georgie sat up and rubbed his hand over Greg's arm. "How come you gots too much hair on your arms?"

Greg quickly looked at Miss Huntley, slightly embarrassed by Georgie's question. Then he chuckled and turned to Georgie. "What do you mean, too much?"

"Well, **you** know, like a monkey. How come you gots that much?"

Greg knew his face had turned red. He smiled. "I don't know. Maybe . . . maybe because God gave it to me that way." Georgie nodded his head, indicating he was satisfied with Greg's response.

"Did God give ya a moustache, too?" Georgie craned his neck to see Greg's moustache and then stood to gently brush his finger across the bristly hair.

"Yes, I suppose so."

"Why?"

"Well . . . I guess because God gave me a brain to make decisions, and I decided to grow a moustache."

"Oh." Georgie nodded thoughtfully at Greg and turned toward the TV. Greg grinned at Miss Huntley. He then looked at little Georgie watching TV. A shiver took Greg by surprise and it made his back muscles quiver. Did he really know what he was doing or getting into? Suddenly, into his life had walked this little person who was relying on **him** for answers to questions.

There were so many things Greg needed to do and to think about. He had an appointment that night which he would have to cancel. There were groceries to buy, and Georgie needed clothes immediately. He would also have to enroll Georgie in first grade on Monday morning.

Miss Huntley had described Georgie's case history only briefly earlier that day on the telephone. He knew that Georgie's mother had never married and no one was certain about the natural father. He knew that Georgie's mother had some problems which affected her keeping Georgie. He also knew this was Georgie's first foster home.

Miss Huntley moved toward the door. She turned to

Georgie smiling and gave him a reassuring wink. "I'm sure you'll both get along just fine."

"No!" Georgie yelled and scrambled to his feet. Tears clouded his bright eyes as he ran to clutch tightly to Miss Huntley. "I don' wanna stay, I don' wanna stay!" Miss Huntley knelt down and Georgie pressed his little body against her. He cried so strenuously that it made him gag. "I want my mommy! Oh, please! I want my mom-my. Why don' she come git me?" Georgie stepped abruptly away from Miss Huntley and rubbed his tear-filled eyes. "I promise I'll be good . . . I promise."

Greg knelt down before Georgie. He had to force away a lump that had formed in his throat. What trauma! thought Greg. How could a six-year-old understand these circumstances? What rationale could possibly be used? Suddenly, life seemed so unfair.

"Georgie," Miss Huntley said lovingly, "you're a good boy." She took a Kleenex from her purse and gently wiped Georgie's cheeks. "Remember what we talked about earlier? Your mommy isn't feeling well right now and she needs to rest a lot. You haven't done anything wrong. She just needs some time to get back on her feet."

Sympathetically, Greg reached out to touch Georgie's arm again. Georgie flinched. "Do you know what?" Greg said brightly, not giving Georgie time to respond. "We're going to have to do some shopping."

"Shopping?" Georgie replied in a perky tone.

"Yep. We've got to get you some clothes. How 'bout that?"

"Oh, neat," Georgie responded, becoming more curious. "What kinda clothes? Ya mean like a football jersey? Or a football?" Georgie grinned slightly, his blue eyes sparkling.

Miss Huntley giggled and roughed Georgie's hair. "A football isn't exactly clothing."

"Yeah, but ya see, mine busted," Georgie retorted seriously and turned to face Greg. "Can I git a football?" he asked meekly.

"Well, we'll see," Greg smiled. "Let's just take one thing at a time."

Miss Huntley broke into the conversation, finding it a positive time for her to exit. "Well, gentlemen. I can tell that you both have many places to go and many things to do; so I'd better be on my way." She glanced at Georgie, making sure of his reaction. Georgie's head jerked nervously. Again, Greg reached for Georgie's arm and lightly patted his shoulder.

Miss Huntley smiled at Georgie and nodded her head confidently. Georgie grinned and then hugged her firmly. "Please, Greg, call me if you need to, okay?"

Greg closed the door behind Miss Huntley. A terrifying feeling gripped him in his stomach. Could he handle this? What had he done? What had he gotten himself into? He was a foster parent!

Greg looked at Georgie. Such a beautiful child. And whatever circumstances his mother faced, who could just give away a son? What kind of person could or would do that? How desperate must someone be? Who could just give away another human being . . . like an old, broken toy?

Chapter 2

Greg felt proud, roaming through the department store with Georgie, fussing over what clothes to buy him. He felt very parental, taking Georgie's hand so he would not touch or break anything. While passing other shoppers, Greg wanted to say to them, "Why, yes, he's my boy. Isn't he wonderful?" And Georgie even had physical traits resembling him—blond hair, blue eyes, and a dark complexion. Greg's thoughts shifted to his dear Trudi. Why couldn't she be here to see Georgie? Trudi would have given him so much love. How he longed for her gentleness.

Greg cleared his mind of Trudi when Georgie pointed out loudly to the saleslady an article of clothing he liked. In fact, he had talked constantly since leaving home. The saleslady was helpful while Georgie tried on an assortment of jeans, shirts, and shoes. They also purchased underwear, socks, pajamas, and a winter coat. Greg had not been shopping since Trudi died. But now, material things had taken on a new meaning. Of course he himself didn't have need for a large quantity of clothes. Working at home, he usually wore jeans, knit shirts, and tennis shoes. He owned a couple of nice, dressy outfits for church and for making presentations of finished house designs to clients. He sold designs mainly to established builders and did some private designs for individuals.

It was at the grocery store that Georgie started to get sleepy. The checkout lane was crowded. But, crowded or not, milk, bread, a toothbrush for Georgie, and staples for the cupboard were needed. Being single, Greg usually ate at restaurants or sometimes not at all. He hated eating alone in the emptiness of his mobile home. He detested the loneliness of his life and the ache when he thought of Trudi. Greg still had not accepted the fact that Trudi was dead—a victim of a drunken driver. Why did she have to die? Greg had asked that question to God over and over. She had so much to give. A totally beautiful person, full of life and vigor. Had it only been one year? One week from today they would have been married. Trudi had been more than his fiancee. She had been his best friend since meeting during their junior year of college. Everything reminded Greg of Trudi—the new beginnings of each of the four seasons, music they had listened to together, the Bible they had read together.

"Sir, sir!" Greg jumped as the clerk called to him. Immediately, he turned around to look for Georgie. Georgie was staring up at him, looking puzzled at his preoccupation.

"Oh, sorry," he answered apologetically. "It's been one of those days, I guess." Greg paid the clerk and she handed him the sack of groceries.

"Can I carry the stuff? I gots muscles." Georgie grinned and reached for the large sack. It was practically as big as he!

"Okay." Greg raised an eyebrow apprehensively.

"But kind of hold the bottom so it won't tear."

"He'll be fine." The clerk smiled and winked at Georgie. Georgie walked toward the exit door. "Your little boy is a doll. How old is he?"

Greg answered without hesitation. "Oh, he's six." Greg suddenly realized the meaning of his response to the clerk. She had assumed Georgie was his boy. "Oh, but he's not my—" Greg stopped. What did it matter? After all, Georgie **was** his foster son. And, legally, he was his guardian. Greg continued, "He hasn't had his birthday this year. He'll be seven this summer—in July."

Driving to the mobile home court, Greg thought how different it was to come home with another person. Life would certainly be different now than it had been being alone. It seemed exciting to think about cooking and caring for someone else's interests besides his own. The mobile home took on a drastically different meaning. It wasn't just three bedrooms, a bath, a kitchen, and a living room, surrounded on the outside by tall pine trees. It was home—home for Georgie and him. Greg got a happy chill as he thought how he could live for someone again. He was tired of thinking how much he missed Trudi, and it was time to give to others.

Greg rummaged for the door key, while trying to balance a sack of clothes and a bag of groceries. Many times he had tried to convince himself it was time to give to others, time to get his life back in order. Trudi whisked into his thoughts again, like a sharp, slicing knife. Would he **ever** succeed in convincing himself? Greg felt weary from his mind changing back and forth. Suddenly, his skeptical thoughts seemed to burst, as the key dropped to the damp porch. "Blast it," Greg muttered to himself, momentarily forgetting Georgie's presence. He quickly smiled at Georgie and opened the door.

Once inside and settled, Greg fixed toasted cheese

sandwiches and tomato soup. It was a cold evening and the hot soup tasted good. After their meal, Greg helped Georgie with a much-needed bath and shampoo. Georgie splashed in the water, having the time of his life. Judging from the dirty water, it had been several days since his last bath.

Georgie was exhausted. It had been a long afternoon and evening. As Georgie climbed into his bed, he saw some children's books on the headboard. Greg kept a few toys and books around the house for when his niece and nephew visited from out of town. Tired as he was, Georgie wanted a bedtime story read to him. Greg gave in happily.

"How about the story of Saul?" asked Greg. Georgie nodded.

"He's the one who drives race cars, ain't he?"

"No, not quite," Greg smiled. "Here, listen. I'll read it to you."

"Will ya read it twice?"

"I haven't read it once yet," Greg teased. "Better not. It's been a busy day. I'll read it again to you some other time."

"Okay, but do I get a snack? I'm hungry."

"We'll do that tomorrow night. It's getting late, and besides, we just ate. It's time for all little boys to go to bed—and sleep. Do you want to hear the story about Saul?"

"Yeah."

"Good. Now listen carefully."

"But can I tell ya somethin' first?"

"Okay," Greg sighed wearily.

"I gotta go to the baf-room."

"Okay, hurry."

Georgie was quickly back in bed. Greg sat on the edge of the bed and read the story. After reading, he leaned over and kissed Georgie on the cheek.

Georgie's eyes widened in surprise. "How come ya did that?" he exclaimed in a squeaky voice, obviously embarrassed.

"Did what?" Greg responded, equally as shocked at Georgie's reaction, but knowing what Georgie meant. He wanted to gather Georgie in his arms and say, "That's okay, little Georgie. I'll take care of you. Don't be afraid. It's an ugly world out there, but you're safe here."

"How come ya kissed me?"

"I just wanted to let you know that I'm happy you're here and that you're welcome here. Is that okay?"

Georgie grinned, his eyes turned toward the wall. "That's okay," he said softly.

"Good night, Georgie. Sleep tight, and don't let the bedbugs bite. Tomorrow we'll go to church."

"Ya mean where they sing and stuff?"

"Right, and pray, too."

"But do I hafta sing and pray?"

"Well, we'll see when we get there. I think you'll like it. Now, pleasant dreams. See you in the morning." Greg tucked the covers around Georgie. He turned off the bedroom light and switched on a night light in the hallway.

Becoming a father felt so good to Greg. He liked feeling that someone was dependent on him, that he was needed. And he wanted to make Georgie feel that he was needed too. If only Trudi and he could have married and had a family. It wasn't fair! He had loved her so much, and she him. Bitterness swept over Greg, as a rush of blood instantly tensed his muscles. That old drunk! That disgusting old drunk! He is alive—off the hook—and she is dead.

Greg took off his shoes and changed to his bathrobe. He curled up on the sofa and listened to some Mozart on the stereo. It was soothing to his soul. He noticed the Bible on the coffee table before him. It reminded him that he and Trudi had often prayed together. Oh, if only his faith would return! If only he could pray again. If only Trudi was alive. Tears blurred Greg's eyes. He wept softly into the pillow on the sofa. "I need you, Trudi," he whispered. "You are the only one, I love you . . . I love you."

"Greg." A tiny voice called from the hallway. It was Georgie.

Greg was startled by the voice at first, then realized it had been quite some time ago that Georgie went to bed. He quickly wiped his eyes. "What's the matter, Georgie?"

"I can't sleep . . . and can I ask ya somethin'?"

"You really should be sleeping," Greg answered in a fatherly tone. He glanced at the alarm clock for Georgie's benefit. "It's way past your bedtime. Ask me quickly. What is it?"

"Well, what I wanted to know is how come all those old guys can hear God talk and we can't?"

"What old guys? Have you been dreaming, Georgie?"

"No, ya know, like Saul in that story. Hey! Why are your eyes all red?"

Greg sniffed and deliberately rubbed his eyes. "Gettin' a little cold, I guess."

"Well, anyways. I tried to talk to God jus' now, you know, like that one old guy."

"You mean Saul," Greg concluded, interrupting Georgie.

"Yeah, Saul. But God didn't answer me. How come He didn't answer me?"

Georgie curled up on the sofa beside Greg. "God heard you, Georgie. He really did." Greg paused, wondering how he could explain to Georgie something **he** was struggling with so deeply. He knew he believed in God. But in the last year it was increasingly harder for him to understand why Trudi died. He did not blame God . . . or did he? He did not attend church regularly or read his Bible or pray.

"I guess if you believe in God, you just have to **know** that he hears your prayers and questions. It's called having faith in God." Greg searched for something more to say. "What did you ask God, Georgie?"

Georgie did not answer immediately. He slowly lowered his head as if in shame. "Oh, jus' if I wouldn't be scared in that sleepin' room . . . you know, of the dark and all . . . an' . . . an—" A sudden heave of Georgie's shoulders and chest launched a hysterical convulsion of tears. Georgie began wailing, "I want my mommy," over and over. Greg held Georgie in his arms, rocking slowly. He felt so helpless. A boy needed his mother. What was **he** to do?

"I'm really sorry," whispered Greg. "Please don't cry."

Greg rocked Georgie gently for several minutes. Gradually, short whimpers replaced the crying and Greg turned Georgie to face him.

"You don't have to be afraid, Georgie. God loves you . . . and I'm right here, too." Greg smiled at Georgie reassuringly. "Here, let's go tuck you back in bed and we'll pray together."

Georgie looked at Greg, his eyes red from crying. He stretched out his arms to be held and Greg carried him to bed.

"Let's close our eyes and pray. Dear Lord, thank you for hearing us, loving us, caring for us, and keeping us safe like you did Saul. And thank you for Georgie. Amen."

"Amen," Georgie echoed in an innocent confidence. "And can I tell ya somethin'?"

"Sure, Georgie."

"I don't feel scared no more."

"Good, I'm glad. Now sleep tight. See you in the

mornin'.''

"Can I tell ya somethin' else?''

"Georgie. Tomorrow's another day. **Now** it's time for sleep.''

"Oh **please**! I promise. Jus' one more thing!''

"Just one. But that's all, because I'm going to bed too.''

"Come 'ere,'' Georgie smiled slightly. Greg knelt beside him. "I like you. Do you like me?''

Greg smiled. "Yes, Georgie, I like you.'' Greg left Georgie's room and picked up his Bible in the living room. He went to his bedroom and knelt beside the bed.

He clasped his hands and thoughtfully rested his chin on them. God works in mysterious ways, thought Greg. There were some selfish reasons for wanting a foster child. But that seemed okay, because Georgie needed him as much as he needed Georgie. Trudi's absence and his loneliness were real to him. God must have placed this little boy in his home for a purpose. Could that be? Could God have placed Georgie in his home as an instrument to help him gain new faith?

Greg opened his Bible to Psalm 51. It was a favorite Psalm he had read many times. He read it aloud quietly. "Create in me a clean heart, O God, and put a new and right spirit within me. Cast me not away from thy presence, and take not thy Holy Spirit from me. Restore to me the joy of thy salvation, and uphold me with a willing spirit. Then I will teach transgressors thy ways, and sinners will return to thee.''

Greg slipped into his bed and stretched under the covers. "Dear Father, thank you for Your Son, Jesus. And thank you for second chances. Create in me a clean heart, O God, and put a new and right spirit within me. Amen.''

The cold March night air chilled the mobile home. Greg pulled the covers around his shoulders. His head sank into the clean, fluffy pillow. For the first time in months, he felt a deep sense of inner peace. For the first time in months, there was something or someone else to think about and care for besides his self-pity. For the first time in months, he could sleep—peacefully, without interruption.

Chapter 3

The smell of freshly perked coffee filled the mobile home. Greg poured some into a large mug and reclined in a living room chair. It had snowed during the night, and about five inches had accumulated. All was peaceful and quiet.

Greg meditated over the reading of Psalm 51 just a few hours earlier. "Create in me a clean heart," he mumbled softly. Spontaneously, Greg dropped to his knees. His hands clenched in a hopeful outreach for an inner peace. "God . . . I . . . I hurt so much. I can't stand it any longer. I hate so much too, Lord. And I envy people who are happy. I can't stand to go up and down and back and forth like this—" Greg turned his body and rested his arms and head on the chair cushion. Silent tears followed.

Just as spontaneously as Greg had fallen to his knees, he sat up on the chair and thoughtfully sipped his black coffee. What was it in him that retained the past? On the other hand, what was it that made him compassionate enough to want to see a six-year-old find comfort and happiness?

Losing his own parents a year apart from each other **was** a strong force. But that had happened in his college years—a much different situation than Georgie's. And he was so grateful for Doris. Having an older sister had helped many times in growing up, especially after his parents' deaths.

Then there was Trudi. Greg gulped hard, again focusing in on the realization of her death and his loneliness. But it had been comforting to know that, whenever he felt the impulse, he could drive the 150-mile trip to see Doris, Randy and the kids, to get his mind off Trudi.

"Sometimes, Lord, I find it hard to praise You and to say 'thank you,' but I do feel moved to thank You for my family. I could never have made it even this far without them. Thank you. I know I fall short a lot, Lord. Please let it be Your will to pick me up again."

Greg decided he would have to see Doris and Randy again soon. Justin was four and Tracy was two. He thought Georgie might profit from getting to know them—a new, ready-made family for Georgie.

Greg walked down the hallway and peeked into Georgie's room. He was excited about getting on with the fathering, and he wished Georgie would wake up. The first full day for Georgie in his new home had to be perfect, perfect for "his little boy."

Janet Huntley had told Greg, during their earlier conversations, that Georgie possibly had no exposure to church. He felt good that Miss Huntley had mentioned that, more out of Christian concern than professional concern. He thought that, even though Georgie lacked exposure to church, he appeared to be a deep thinker, with all the talk of God and prayer. He was anxious for Georgie to experience so many things. Poor kid, Greg pondered. Some children never have hope in life. And this was just one little boy! So many children were neglected, in so many ways.

Soon Georgie was stirring around in his room, puting on his new underwear and clothes. "Can I put my new brown shoes on for church?" Georgie shouted to Greg.

"Yes, Georgie," Greg shouted back, equally as loud.

"Hey, Gr-eg," Georgie shouted again as Greg entered his bedroom. "I ain't got no socks!"

"You ain't got no socks?" Greg copied Georgie in a teacher-like fashion, calling attention to poor grammar.

"That's right. They ain't in my drawer," Georgie acknowledged and pointed inside the drawer, entirely missing Greg's hint.

"No, Georgie. What I meant was, you don't have **any** socks."

"That's what I said. I ain't got no socks, see?" Again Georgie pointed inside the drawer. Greg laughed. Georgie obviously did not understand Greg's subtle correction. He showed Georgie his socks hidden beneath the underwear.

"Guess I didn't look good enough, huh?"

"Well, I'm proud of you for getting dressed without being told. It's going to take some getting used to around here before you remember where everything is." Greg patted him on the back. "Your new clothes really look great! You're a handsome boy, Georgie Stainer."

Georgie blushed. "They feel good, too." Georgie smelled the fabric of his new shirt. "And they smell like that store we was in."

"We **were** in," Greg corrected.

"That's what I said," Georgie stammered. Greg laughed inwardly.

Shoveling the sidewalk to the car and cleaning the snow off the car was a twenty-minute affair. Georgie wanted to help, but he was already dressed for church and Greg did not want him to get wet. So Georgie stayed inside, attempting to put a puzzle together.

The tires on Greg's little green MG sports car spun on the fresh snow and ice. Soon they were driving on the narrow county road to his church in town.

"This must be a used car," Georgie said matter-of-factly and pointed to the gear shift boot on the floor.

"What makes you think that?"

" 'Cause that black thing's all wrinkled."

"No, Georgie. It's supposed to be that way. See?" Greg shifted gears to show him the flexibility of the rubber gear shift boot.

"Can I do that?"

"You mean, **may** I do that."

"Okay," Georgie sighed in a resigned manner. "**May** I do that?"

"Better not. It's too slippery and snowy on the road. Maybe in the summer when the roads are dry."

"Sum-mer?" Georgie straightened up in the bucket seat. His face screwed up in perplexity. "I won't be here that long. Janet said as soon as my mom was feelin' better I could go home." Georgie sounded defensive and his squeaky voice trembled.

Greg felt helpless again and at a loss for comforting words. "Well . . . whenever you leave, I'll make sure you get to help shift the gears some other time when the roads are clear." The blank look on Georgie's face indicated he no longer had any interest in shifting gears. An unsureness of how long or by what circumstances Georgie's stay would be, made Greg uncomfortable in answering his statement. Greg decided a telephone call to Janet Huntley in the morning would be in order.

As they approached the church, Greg pointed up at the gigantic steeple, hovering in the sky like a sturdy rocket.

"Is **that** your **church?**" Georgie craned his neck to see the steeple. He was in awe of the enormity of the towering mass of bricks. "Are there bells in that thing?"

"Sure. Listen." Greg again pointed upward. "They're ringing now."

Greg pulled into a parking space and turned off the motor. Georgie rolled the window part way down so he could hear better. Freezing winter air and a gust of wind rushed into the small car. Georgie let out a "Neat-o," then quickly rolled up the window.

As the pair entered the front door, they could hear the enormous pipe organ. The organist was playing a prelude that rumbled through the huge gothic structure with bold reverence. The morning sunlight sparkled through the stained glass rose window located high above the altar. Georgie stared at the glittering rays and spoke a soft unconscious "Oooh."

A few "good mornings" were exchanged with acquaintances, as were a few "Who's that with Greg?" stares. Then Greg chose a pew about halfway to the front.

People in the congregation reached for their hymnals as the organist played an introductory verse to "Glorious Things of Thee Are Spoken." Georgie reached for a hymnal, too. Greg started to help him find the page number. But, as he did that, Georgie pulled the hymnal to his chest as if he wanted to find it himself. In the middle of the third verse he finally let Greg show him the right page.

Greg watched Georgie out of the corner of his eye. Georgie only knew a few basic sight words, so he started singing "la-la-la" at the top of his lungs. How could such a little kid have such a penetrating voice? People were turning around in their pews to look, some smiling and some **not** smiling. But Georgie was unaware of anyone around him. His face beamed with delight at what he found inside this building—a place he had a right to be but possibly never had been before.

Greg did not want to interrupt this precious moment for Georgie, although his singing was a bit loud. So he patted Georgie lightly on the knee. Georgie looked up at Greg and quieted down but continued with "la-la-la," this time not quite as loudly.

After the hymn, Georgie leaned to Greg, cupped his hands and whispered in his ear. "Is this where they give ya blood to drink?" Greg frowned as if not hearing Georgie's question. "I said, is this where they give ya blood to drink? My friend Jim, he's eight, says ya drink blood in church." Georgie wrinkled his nose, shook his head, stuck out his tongue, and acted as if he were gagging.

Greg's first reaction was to grab Georgie's arm and squeeze.

"Ouch!" Georgie shouted. Could this really be happening? thought Greg. Everyone (or it seemed like everyone) was turning around to see what was going on. He was mortified!

Georgie jerked back, shaking the pew, his lower lip protruding, and whispered, "Ya hurt my arm!"

"I'm sorry. But please sit still and don't talk. I'll answer your questions about church later."

"But all I wanted ta know was if ya drink blood in church."

"Ssssh, no! Now quiet, **please.**"

Previously, everytime Greg saw children writing or drawing in church, it annoyed him that parents had to pacify them in that way. But now, he could understand better. During the sermon, he handed Georgie the Sunday bulletin and a pen. Georgie promptly accepted and immediately calmed down. He was a "little angel" the remainder of the service.

Upon leaving the church, the people were surprised to find that it was snowing very hard, and the wind had drifted the roads. At least groceries were bought yesterday, thought Greg. If it continued to snow, there probably would not be any school the next day. That was something he had not worried about previously. School closings! In fact, because of working primarily in his home, snow hardly affected him. Now suddenly, overnight, school closings were an issue in his life.

Greg cleaned the new accumulation of snow from his car. Sometimes he wished he lived in Florida instead of in northern Indiana's snow belt. Snow was fine . . . when you could stay inside.

On the way home, Georgie repeated his question about drinking blood in church. Greg attempted to give a brief, elementary explanation of communion. Greg soon found out that first grade kids have a short attention span, as he saw Georgie peer out the window at a huge snowplow passing by.

Fried chicken, mashed potatoes, broccoli, rolls, milk, mixed fruit, and cookies—this was the menu Greg had planned for Sunday dinner. He stood at the kitchen counter trying to decide how or what to do first. So far in Georgie's short stay, he had been a parent, counselor, and disciplinarian. And now he was the family cook. The thought of that made Greg laugh to himself.

As Georgie watched another church service, "of all things," on TV, Greg prepared the meal. He thought he had prepared more meals in the last two days than he had prepared for himself in the last two weeks.

"Do you know any prayers to say before lunch?" Greg walked over to Georgie in the living room and switched off the TV.

"Nope."

Greg took Georgie's hand and led him to the kitchen

table. "Then I'll say the prayer today, and you listen real hard and try to learn it." Georgie quickly slid the chair away from the table and sat down. Greg began praying slowly so Georgie could follow. "God is great and God is good. Let us thank Him for our food. By His hands we all are fed; give us Lord our daily bread. Amen."

Georgie ate his food item by item—all the mashed potatoes and rolls, all the chicken, and so on. He ate the broccoli last, making terrible faces of dislike, and then washed it down with milk. He gulped, snorted, wheezed, smacked, and slurped. Such a sight! Never in his life had he used a knife and fork to any extent. That was very obvious.

"Slow down, Georgie," scolded Greg. "You're making me eat fast just watching you," he said, using the phrase that his mother had used on him many times while growing up. "There's plenty more; you don't have to gulp. It's not good for your digestive system."

"My what?"

"Your stomach."

"Oh."

Within seconds, Georgie was stuffing himself again. He asked for more food and repeated the routine.

"Ya know that preacher I was watching on TV?" Georgie popped a cookie into his already-full mouth.

"Yes. And don't eat the cookies yet; they're for dessert."

"He's the one my mom watches sometimes. She says ya don't gotta go to church if ya watch it on TV. How come ya go if ya don't gotta?"

"Because I like to go, I guess. And please, Georgie, don't talk with your mouth full of food."

"Do I gotta go if I watch it on TV?"

"Why? Didn't you like church this morning?"

Georgie nodded his head and stuffed half a buttered roll in his mouth. Greg frowned at Georgie for his piggishness. "Oh yeah. I really liked it, but—"

"But what?"

"Can I ask ya somethin'?"

"You **may** ask me something."

Georgie smiled at Greg's correction. "**May** I have another roll, please?"

"Since you asked so politely, yes. But only if you promise not to stuff it in your mouth like the last one."

"I promise." Georgie giggled, as Greg buttered a roll for him.

"So anyway, what was it you were going to tell me about church?" There was a long pause. Georgie was hesitant in answering the question, as if he had changed his mind. Greg hoped he wasn't pushing him, but he was curious about what was bothering Georgie. By this time, Georgie was getting fidgety in his chair.

"Do I hafta tell ya?" Georgie whined.

"No. I just thought you might want to. If there is something bothering you, I'll be glad to listen and try to help you with it."

"Promise ya won't laugh?"

"I wouldn't think of it, Georgie."

"Double promise?"

"Double promise. It will be just between you and me. Our secret." Greg reached for the little, serious Georgie and sat him on his lap. Suddenly, Georgie started talking very fast, turning his head away from Greg as if to get it all out in the open quickly.

"Well . . . I don't like spirits. An' my friend Jim, he's eight, said there's all kinds of scary spirits, an' the preacher this morning in church was talkin' about spirits, an' my friend Jim who's eight says those old spirits will haunt you when you're sleepin' at night an' drive ya crazy an' all the people that died will be there too, an' haunt me an' try to kill me an' . . ."

Georgie finally took a long breath. He **was** listening this morning in church, even while drawing, thought Greg. The minister had been talking about the Holy Spirit dwelling within people.

"Georgie, the minister this morning was talking about the **Holy** Spirit. The Holy Spirit is a good spirit. He's the Spirit of God, the God we pray to. He lives in us so we can tell people about God and live happy and good lives." It seemed strange to Greg, as it had Saturday, that he was telling things about God to another person—things that he had lost faith in. Trudi was with her Heavenly Father . . . he knew that. That was his one great consolation.

"Ya mean the good spirit won't hurt me?"

"Of course not. In fact, you don't have to be afraid of evil spirits if you have the Holy Spirit in you."

"How d'ya know if ya have Him?"

"Just ask God for Him, Georgie. Just ask for the Holy Spirit to come into your life and heart, and then thank Jesus." Greg gave Georgie a light squeeze. Georgie giggled excitedly, appearing to be pleased at the new information he had acquired.

Georgie swallowed the last of his buttered roll and lightly hugged Greg. "Ya know what?" Georgie's voice squeaked softly.

"What?"

"You're jus' like a daddy, I think." Georgie looked up at Greg in wonder. Georgie then said matter-of-factly, raising his voice, "I don't have a daddy, ya know. You're my daddy; okay, Daddy?"

Greg decided that that was Georgie's way of asking, "Can I call ya daddy?" And what would it hurt? After all, he needed a dad. That is why he was here. He needed a home, not just a foster home. If only Trudi could have heard the conversation, she would have been proud and excited.

"Sure, Georgie. You call me 'Daddy.' And do you know what?" Greg lightly touched Georgie's little nose. "I think you're a pretty neat kid."

All that afternoon and evening, and through the night, the snow fell steadily. The cold wind blew hard, like a giant, rotary ceiling fan, constantly and evenly. But all was warm in the mobile home—warm and secure for Georgie.

Chapter 4

Just as Greg had predicted, the announcer on the morning radio news reported that all county schools were closed. His first thoughts were of trudging through the snow to the car and heading for town to have coffee with the local cronies. "I can't do that," Greg mused, then laughed to himself for momentarily forgetting the new addition to the family. It seemed like a small thing to have to give up, yet many times a few cups of coffee in the morning with friends had started his day in a good direction. But, in a way, it was nice to have one more full day to get to know Georgie.

Greg thought it would be good if Georgie slept a little longer, since it had been a busy weekend. A peaceful cup of coffee in the solitude of his own home would suffice. It would give him time to think of the drawings or blueprints he was going to work on that day. And it was high time to start! Where had the weekend gone? Usually he spent several hours drawing on Saturdays. Drawing wasn't work to him; it was a way of life.

Greg opened the door to his office. It was cold and damp from being closed all weekend. The heat vent was shut. Usually, Greg left it closed and kept the door open. That made the room just the right temperature. He liked it cool when he worked.

Greg sat down and peered at the accumulation of papers before him. The drafting table had the same prints clipped to it as it had on Saturday morning when Janet Huntley had called. "Is Greg Larwell home, please?"

"Yes, this is Greg Larwell speaking," he recalled saying Saturday when he answered the telephone.

"This is Janet Huntley from the County Welfare Department. I think we've found a little boy for you, finally. I know it's been a long time that you've waited. But we just didn't feel that we had the right match until now."

Greg had been stunned. His heart beat rapidly. Should he make an excuse right away that he was too busy now, or that he had changed his mind? He was excited, but could he handle it? "Go on," Greg had said in a cautious tone.

"His name is Georgie Stainer. We need a home for him right away. We took him away from his mother because of some problems. He is six years old and an only child, plus his real father's identity is not known. His mother was never married."

The moment had come! Greg panicked. Should he take the child? He had found himself sitting at the kitchen table, his foot tapping nervously up and down on the floor.

"Well . . . when is 'right away'? I mean, do you mean right now?"

"Yes, I'm afraid so, at least in a couple of hours."

After an uncomfortable pause, Greg had heard himself say, "Yes, bring him over."

As Greg straightened up the prints on the drafting table

he recalled running through the house that Saturday like a marathon runner, dusting furniture and washing three days' worth of dishes!

Greg sipped his coffee, pondering his life. It was so compact up until now. Getting ahead in the world was his main ambition. Since Trudi's death, his goals turned to making good money, lots of money, to get ahead.

"Oh, God," he whispered. "I know I don't talk to You much anymore. And I know I should." He glanced out the window at the peaceful snow-covered field across the road. "What peace, Lord. Your creation is so peaceful. I'm Your creation too, and I need peace. Where's it all going? What's in store for me? I have enough problems without Georgie; what's he here for—? Help me, Lord, to put things in proper perspective. I want to serve You. Show me how."

Faint hints of sunshine squeezed their way through the shutters. The snow had completely stopped, and the fields across the road gave the impression of a rolling, sandy desert.

Perfect conditions to work, thought Greg, busily collecting drafting tools he would need to finish the drawings. Another day of work and the Whitney contract would be completed. Skillfully, he started measuring, computing, and putting it down on paper. Everything he did was to perfection. In his house, everything was in its place and clean, with the exception of dirty dishes which he detested washing.

An hour passed by quickly, and it was almost eight-thirty. Georgie still had not awakened. So Greg started to prepare breakfast—Spam, eggs, toast, and orange juice. The tempting aromas aroused Georgie's senses, for he soon came staggering into the kitchen, yawning and rubbing his eyes.

"What ya makin'?" Georgie asked in an early morning

mumble.

"Spam and eggs. Smell good?"

"Yeah." Georgie walked to the TV set and switched it on. He just stood there in front of the set, groggily staring at Captain Kangaroo.

A soiled smell attracted Greg's attention moments after Georgie's walk through the kitchen. Greg looked at him standing in the living room, his pajamas wrinkled and wet.

"Georgie. Did you wet your bed?"

"No!" Georgie screamed defensively, trying to hide the results of his wetting. "I didn't wet."

"But Georgie, your pajamas are all wet." Greg quickly went into Georgie's bedroom. The sheets and blankets were not on the bed. "Where's your bedding, Georgie?" Greg asked, becoming impatient. By this time, Georgie was standing in the bedroom doorway.

"It's in the drawer," he said meekly.

"What? Whatever for? If you wet your bed, the sheets should go in the bathtub until we can wash them!"

Georgie ran to the bathroom crying. Greg followed close behind, feeling like a heel.

"I didn't mean to make you feel badly, Georgie. It's just that, if you have a problem with wetting the bed, you need to tell me about it, not hide it."

Greg helped Georgie change to dry clothes. Suddenly, the smell of burning food filtered through the house, and Greg ran to the kitchen to find burnt Spam and eggs. Fortunately, he had not toasted the bread. He cleaned the pan, made fresh Spam and eggs, and they were soon eating happily.

Janet Huntley had not mentioned Georgie having a problem with bed-wetting. Maybe she didn't know because of him being a foster child for the first time. Greg was relieved that he had purchased a washer and dryer several months before. Next to hating to wash dishes, he hated laundry establishments.

After breakfast, Greg instructed Georgie on how to dry dishes. One cracked glass and one broken dish later, they were done. Georgie had enjoyed helping. He said it was "hard work," and dusted his hands together several times, as if wanting praise.

"You're a good worker, Georgie. You can help me a lot around the house." Greg tried to exaggerate a bit, hoping it would compensate for making him feel ashamed in the bed-wetting episode.

"Can I shovel the snow? Look!" He pointed to the sidewalk Greg had shoveled Sunday morning. "Oh, please! It's covered with snow. It must be a thousand trillion feet deep! Hey! When do I go to school?"

"I haven't had a chance to tell you. They called off school today. You'll probably have school tomorrow."

Georgie looked disappointed, but was happy when Greg got the shovel from the closet inside the front door. It was a fifteen-minute process for Georgie to get all his winter wraps on. Then he took the shovel and walked out into the cold, looking determined to please Greg. Greg knelt on the living room chair and watched Georgie through the window for a few minutes. Methodically, section by section, Georgie shoveled his way to the car.

While Georgie shoveled snow for twenty minutes, Greg took advantage of the time and worked on the Whitney contract. Soon he heard a tiny knock on the front door. There stood Georgie, covered from head to toe with snow, soaking wet. According to Georgie, he had made angels in the snow.

"Georgie! You are drenched! We've got to get you out of those wet clothes immediately. You'll catch a cold."

Once changed, Georgie withdrew to his bedroom to "fix it up." What little possessions he had, he made good use of. Georgie moved the small bed and night stand, rearranged his clothes in the drawers and closet, and taped a snapshot of his mother to the wall.

"Hey, Grr-egg . . . come see what I done in my room!" Georgie quickly corrected himself. "I mean . . . Daddy."

Daddy? The new name temporarily stopped Greg in his tracks. It sounded good. He smiled and drew back his shoulders slightly. He would have to get used to it, but somehow he thought it would not take long.

Greg walked down the narrow hallway. Having heard the sounds of furniture moving, he expected to find chaos. But, to his surprise, everything was nicely arranged. He was amazed at the pride Georgie took in wanting things to look good. Was Georgie's mother like that? Did she train him to put things in order?

"Super, Georgie! Everything really looks great." Greg's eyes fixed on the snapshot taped to the wall and walked closer to examine it.

"Is this your mommy?" Greg tried to sound as natural and positive as he could. The photo was wrinkled and torn. The woman appeared to be in her late thirties or early forties. Her face looked tough, full of lines.

"Yeah, that's her. She's pretty, ain't she? I can see her sometime; that's what the caseworker said. When can I see her?"

"Yes, sure Georgie. I'll have to talk with Janet Huntley and find out about that."

"When are you goin' ta talk to her?"

"Tomorrow, after I enroll you in school, if you have school. But I suppose you will. It's not snowing or blowing anymore. I'll see her as soon as I drop you off at school, okay?"

"Okay. Hey! What am I goin' ta do **now**?"

"What do you mean?"

"I don't feel like playing in the snow anymore."

"I really don't want you to anyway. The snow is turning sort of slushy. You'd get too wet again. Why don't you finish putting that puzzle together that you started yesterday? Or, you could play with the toys in the toy box, or read a book."

"Hey." Georgie pulled an *Uncle Wiggily* game from the toy box. "Will ya play this game with me?"

"Do you know how to play *Uncle Wiggily?*"

"I played it a couple times with my friend, Jim."

"Well, all right. But just for a little while. I have some drawings to do." He felt he was getting behind schedule. The agreement in the Whitney contract called for everything to be completed by tomorrow. But Georgie needed his attention, too. He could finish the drawings tonight.

The day slipped by quickly. It seemed to Greg that all he accomplished was playing games with Georgie, washing dishes, washing clothes, and cleaning things up. It was seven o'clock—time for Georgie's bath and shampoo.

"But I just took a bath yesterday," Georgie protested.

"No, Georgie. That was Saturday. Today is Monday. You need a bath. Just think how hard you worked today!" Greg smiled at Georgie, hoping the little bit of psychology would convince him.

"No!" Georgie stamped his foot on the floor and folded his arms across his chest. "I ain't gonna do it! I don't need a bath!"

"It will only take you five minutes if you hurry. You want to be clean as a whistle for school."

"I ain't taking no bath, and ya can't make me!" Georgie ran to his bedroom and slammed the door.

Greg followed closely behind and went in after Georgie. By this time, Greg was getting aggravated. It was another new situation to handle—another first.

"Now listen here, young man," Greg said, trying to recall how his father would have handled a situation such as this when he was little. "You don't go stomping off when I'm talking to you, **nor** do you slam doors. Now I'm asking you nicely to get into the bathtub. Either that, or there will be no snack tonight."

The word "snack" somehow struck a nerve in Georgie's ear. In no time, Georgie was in the tub, splashing and singing to his heart's content.

After the snack of cookies and milk, it was eight o'clock and Georgie's bedtime. Georgie was quick to forgive and forget, so he readily hugged and kissed Greg goodnight. After a short bedtime prayer, lights were out. Greg thought it was important to pray each night with Georgie, mentioning especially Georgie's mother and his friend, Jim. In a way, it would keep Georgie in touch with them.

Greg was exhausted. Would every day be this tiring? He hoped not. He looked forward to his day tomorrow. Georgie would be in school, and he would be able to get much work done. Greg pulled off his shoes and heaved a relaxed sigh. He sank down on the recliner and stretched his body. He needed to finish the plans for the Whitney contract—just as soon as he rested for ten minutes.

Chapter 5

It felt good to relax. He and Trudi used to go to her parents' home and sit in front of a glowing fire. Sometimes they would roast marshmallows in the fireplace and put them in steaming hot chocolate. They would talk about their life plans, or just sit on the sofa holding each other closely, watching the warm, inviting fire.

Why did things go wrong? They had prayed many times about their relationship. They were so sure it was in God's plan for them to marry, have children, be together for the rest of their lives.

There were times they would disagree—many times. But it always seemed to work out. They recognized each other as individuals and tried to compromise in some situations. They always asked God to intervene as the final word. With so many relationships in the world that are shaky from the start, why was a beautiful relationship based on love and trust ended, even before it had a chance to mature?

Could he love and trust again? Was it God he was afraid

to trust? People tried to console him by saying things like, "You're young. You'll have many chances to find happiness. Just trust." Was it merely trust, or did he need to ask God for a second chance—a new beginning—to love and trust Him again?

As saintly as Trudi was, she constantly sought out God to admonish her. He remembered one particular sunny summer afternoon when they had gone to a county park for a picnic. It was hot, but the humidity was low, and there was a gentle, fresh breeze.

"Look at that tiny wren bathing in the puddle." Trudi pointed to the wren. She talked softly so as not to scare the little creature. "He's refreshing himself the best he knows how. It's sort of like a new start for him. Wouldn't it be nice if we could start afresh so easily?"

Greg reached into the picnic basket for the golden-brown fried chicken Trudi had prepared for their picnic. "I think everything you do is new and fresh. And you don't seem to have to work at it very hard."

"Greg, I think you're prejudiced," Trudi grinned.

"No, really. When I'm with you . . . well, I guess being with you makes me feel whole . . . do you know what I mean?"

"Yes, Greg," Trudi smiled and touched his arm. A gentle breeze blew back her light brown hair. Her smile was radiant. "You know I feel the same way. You really bring out the best in me. I love you, Greg," Trudi whispered.

"I love you. I just can't believe how deeply I love you. I just want to sit and look at you, forever. You're **so** beautiful."

"I'm so happy."

"Come on." Greg stood up and grabbed Trudi's hands, pulling her up. "Let's go on the merry-go-round!"

"But what about our lunch?"

Greg started to run as if racing Trudi to the merry-go-round. "That's okay," he shouted back as he ran. "We have lots of time."

Trudi followed Greg, running, trying to catch up to him. "Do you like to play on the merry-go-round?" Trudi kidded.

"Yeah," Greg laughed. "I think I'm reverting to my childhood."

"That's fine," Trudi said as she took a deep breath and sat down on the merry-go-round. "Sometimes I think that's when we're the closest to God . . . when we're childlike." She situated herself more comfortably on the wooden seat. "Come on, Greg. Push! It was your idea to come over here instead of eating."

Greg changed positions in the recliner. He must try to get Trudi out of his thoughts so he could finish the drawings that were due tomorrow. "Lord . . . I know nothing can separate me from Your love. You never give us too much to bear. I need a new beginning . . . to start where I am. Thank you for Your constant love. I pray that I will be more like You, every hour of every day . . . Thank you, Jesus. Nothing can separate me from the love of God . . ."

Chapter 6

The kitchen clock chimed. One . . . two . . . three . . . Greg rubbed his eyes and extended his arms, stretching. Four . . . five . . . six . . . seven. . . .? "No!" Greg groaned. "It can't be!" Greg jumped up and drew back the drapes. It was! It was morning! How could he have done such a dumb thing? The contract! And Georgie needed to get up for school.

"Time to get up, Georgie. Good morn-ing." Greg lightly shook Georgie's arm. Georgie scowled. "Come on out to breakfast. We have to hurry. I got up a little late. Cheerios okay?"

Not only did little Georgie not like to take baths, he also did not like getting up early. Greg had him wash his face and hands, get dressed, and fold his pajamas. Georgie grumped at every move. He also had Georgie gather up the bed sheets which he had wet again.

Greg poured Georgie's cereal and orange juice, made toast, and hurried to get himself dressed while Georgie ate. A few minutes before eight they left their house for school.

Entering the principal's office, they were greeted by the school secretary. Greg explained his situation to her, and she assigned Georgie to Miss Stevenson's first grade class. While in the office, Greg purchased all the school supplies Georgie would need. Then the secretary escorted them to Miss Stevenson's room—Room 1A.

The 8:10 bell buzzed loudly through the long corridor as the trio approached the classroom. The secretary opened the door and motioned for the teacher to come over. Greg glanced into the room like a nervous father. Miss Stevenson smiled and acknowledged their presence.

Greg could not help staring at Miss Stevenson as she walked toward them. She walked with a gracefulness and had an air of confidence about her. Her dark brown eyes and hair complemented her delicate complexion. He felt awkward, thinking that she might sense his gawking.

"Good morning, Miss Stevenson." The secretary almost sang when she talked. "We have a new student for you this morning. His name is George Stainer. George, this is Miss Stevenson."

"Georg-ie, not George," Georgie said, partly annoyed, but with a certain shyness.

"Oh, I'm sorry. This is Georgie, not George," she corrected gently. "And this is Georgie's foster father, Greg Larwell."

"It's nice to meet you, Georgie, and Mr. Larwell. I'll try to make Georgie feel as comfortable as I can today . . ." Miss Stevenson was distracted with the stirring sounds of children's voices coming from her classroom.

"Oh, yes," the secretary reassured Georgie. "Miss Stevenson will help you get settled and show you around the school. And the kids will help you, too." The secretary smiled and patted Georgie on the shoulder. She started walking down the hallway toward the office and added, "You'll be all right; you're in good hands."

"By the sound of things," Miss Stevenson nodded her head toward the classroom, "I'd better get back in there. Say, instead of Georgie riding the bus home tonight, could you pick him up after school? Then I could take both of you on a tour of the school so you would be familiar with everything. Would that suit you?"

"Sounds like a good idea. What time is school over?"

"At two-thirty."

"Two-thirty? Right, I'll be here." Greg leaned over and turned Georgie toward him. "You be good, Georgie. I'll see you this afternoon."

"I will be," Georgie said timidly.

"There's nothing to worry about," chimed in Miss Stevenson. "I'm sure he will fit right in. The other children are always anxious to meet new playmates. And we're starting a new art project this afternoon. Do you like art, Georgie?" Georgie responded with an anxious nod of his head.

"See you later, Georgie, and thanks, Miss Stevenson." Greg winked at Georgie and started down the hallway. Passing the office area on the way out, he was informed by the secretary that Georgie would need a physical, unless he had had one in the last six months. Since no medical records were available for him, and the county welfare office also required a physical examination, he assured her it would be done in the coming week.

Greg used the pay phone in the hallway to call a local pediatrician's office. Dr. Hill's receptionist put Greg on hold. While waiting, he thought of all the things he had to do. There were so many things! Looking out for someone else was a full-time job in itself. But finishing the contract was an absolute necessity! Today!

The receptionist said there was an opening the next

afternoon at three-thirty because of a cancellation. Perfect, thought Greg. He would pick up Georgie after school and go directly to the doctor's appointment.

At the welfare office, Greg was told Janet Huntley was out on field cases all day. So he made another appointment for eight-thirty the next morning. Good! At least an early appointment would give him most of the next day to work.

By two o'clock that afternoon, Greg had finished the Whitney contract and placed it in a large portfolio. On the way to pick up Georgie he quickly delivered it to his client's office, and shortly after two-thirty he was at the school.

"Hel-lo," Greg called into the classroom. Georgie and his teacher were sitting on the reading rug talking. Greg smiled at Georgie and Miss Stevenson.

"Hello." Miss Stevenson stood up and greeted Greg.

"Everything go okay today?"

"Fine. Georgie made some friends, and I had him say the alphabet for me. He's really good at that." Georgie blushed and grinned widely.

After a fifteen-minute tour of the school, Greg and Miss Stevenson talked quietly just inside the classroom door. In the meantime, Georgie sat at his desk and colored a picture.

"I'm really curious, Mr. Larwell. How and why did you get interested in becoming a foster parent?"

"Well, right now I'm not sure," Greg kidded. "My life certainly has suddenly become very busy. But seriously, I just really like children and I wanted to do something for someone else. And since I'm not married, I thought this would be a good learning experience." Greg nodded his head slightly and then turned his eyes once again to Miss Stevenson. "I don't know yet . . . it's only been a few days. But things seem to be going fine."

"I just don't know how you do it," Miss Stevenson marveled in a soft and amazed tone.

"That makes me think of myself—and teaching," Greg chuckled. "I don't see how you do it. I don't think I could stand it all day long, day in and day out—with all those kids!"

"I manage," Miss Stevenson smiled.

"I'm sure you do," Greg readily agreed. "Come on, Georgie. Let's go home."

Greg had been so busy all day he had not thought about what he was going to make for supper. As a substitute for cooking, he decided to stop at McDonald's for some hamburgers and french fries.

Later at home, it turned into a quiet evening. Georgie enjoyed coloring again with the crayons Greg had bought for him at school, and Greg caught up on some reading. At seven-thirty, Greg made a snack of cheese and crackers.

Greg read Georgie a short story, and then Georgie brushed his teeth, hopped into bed and snuggled under the warm blankets. He looked at Greg and grinned. "Are Miss Stevenson and you goin' to git married?"

"Wh-at? What do you mean, Georgie? I never met her before today."

"Ye-ah but, I saw the way she was making goo-goo eyes at you and you were—"

"All right," Greg laughed and tickled Georgie's stomach. "I think I know someone who's a little goo-goo around **here**. It's time for all Georgies in the world to go to sleep. Do you want to say a prayer tonight?" Georgie shook his head.

"Okay then, I will. Close your eyes." Georgie shut his eyes so tightly it looked as if he were in pain. "Dear Lord, thank you for being with us all the time—while Georgie's at school and when I'm working here at home. Help us to follow you more closely every day. And bless Georgie's mother and his friend Jim. Amen.''

''Can I tell ya somethin'?''

''Sure, Georgie.''

''I love ya, Daddy.''

Greg kissed Georgie's forehead. ''I love you, too, Georgie. Goodnight. Sleep tight.''

''Can I tell ya somethin' else?''

''Hurry. It's sleepin' time.''

''Well, I met this black kid today; his name is Henry. An' we played together at recess, an' he sits beside me in school. He's my friend.''

''That's good, Georgie. Maybe sometime Henry can come over to our house to play. Would you like that?''

Georgie beamed. ''Ye-ah!''

''Okay. Goodnight, Georgie. Pleasant dreams.''

''Goodnight, Daddy, an' ya know what?''

''What Georgie?''

''I think Miss Stevenson is nice.''

''I'm glad you like her, Georgie.''

Chapter 7

Early mornings had not been so routine for Greg since high school—that is, to get up in the morning at a certain time, eat breakfast at a certain time, and now to see a little boy off to school at a certain time.

Getting Georgie up in the morning was becoming increasingly harder, as was the extra work of washing wet sheets. Georgie was definitely not a morning person; although, once fully awake, his disposition changed for the better.

"Here comes the school bus!" Georgie hollered excitedly. He snatched his stocking cap and pulled it snugly down on his head. This would be Georgie's first experience riding a school bus. He giggled as if he were chartered for a world cruise!

"Don't forget, Georgie. Don't ride the school bus home tonight. I'll pick you up right at two-thirty for your doctor's appointment."

"I won't," Georgie called as he ran out the front door. From the window Greg watched Georgie slipping and sliding all the way to the bus.

Greg dressed, fixed a pot of coffee, and relaxed a few minutes before going to the welfare department office. He opened his Bible to the concordance and looked up the word "child." Child rearing was completely new to him. He would appreciate any new inspiration he could get his hands on.

Finding a reference to Proverbs 22:6, he turned to that verse. He read it aloud quickly: "Train up a child in the way he should go, and when he is old he will not depart from it."

He could not have received any better advice. People **pay** to get good advice, and he got it free! Greg laid his Bible on the table and poured a second cup of coffee. "He will not depart from it," Greg recited thoughtfully. But wasn't it true what most psychologists and psychiatrists report, that nothing can be done to change what has been learned in the first years of life?

Of course those years could be damaging **or** productive, Greg reasoned. But how about God . . . and new beginnings? What Georgie needed right now was love—more than anything else. If he could show Georgie love and constructive understanding through Christ, it could be a new beginning for Georgie through the working of the Holy Spirit.

Greg prayed a short prayer thanking God for wisdom and knowledge and understanding. It was nearly time for his appointment with Janet Huntley. Soon he was driving into town to her office.

It had been more than seven months since Greg first sat in the waiting room of the county welfare office. Before, he had felt the anticipation of foster parenthood. Now, he felt the reality of foster parenthood and the sobering thought of responsibility. So many questions had come into his mind. What was Georgie's background? What was going to happen to him? Could he handle keeping Georgie for an extended period of time?

The "not knowing" to the puzzling questions made Greg feel edgy. **His** edginess made him think of Georgie and what anxiety and confusion and uncertainty **he** must be experiencing. Greg hoped he could or had alleviated some of Georgie's fears. Greg breathed deeply. All he could do was trust.

Janet Huntley's office walls were plastered with frames—pictures of children, degrees, awards, and paintings. Her devotion and effectiveness were evident in the scores of children's drawings and snapshots of children patchworked beneath the glass top on her desk.

Miss Huntley closed the office door behind Greg as he seated himself beside her collaged desk. Why was he so nervous? His hands were shaking slightly. Were his questions dumb? Was this visit out of concern for Georgie or satisfaction for himself? Was it both? Why didn't he simply keep Georgie until the welfare department thought it was time for him to go home? Why did he have to know—?

"Now, what can I do for you, Greg?" Miss Huntley sat opposite Greg. "Everything going okay?"

Greg swallowed hard. "Oh, fine!" He tried to camouflage his nervousness by sounding positive. "I . . . I just had a few questions about Georgie."

"I'll be glad to answer what I can."

"Well, it's just that, well . . . it's just that I'm not sure what I'm not or what I am supposed to tell Georgie. Frankly, I don't know, myself."

Miss Huntley smiled and leaned back in her chair. "I'm not sure if I follow you exactly."

"Oh, I'm sorry. I don't know why I'm so nervous. I guess I really care about Georgie, and I don't want to hurt him. What I mean is . . . what should I tell him about going back to his mother, or when? You mentioned that his mother wasn't feeling well, and as soon as she was better he could go back home."

"Yes, well, I'm afraid I'm in the same position as you when it comes to certain cases. When a child asks you questions about "when" and "why," you try to answer them as generally as possible and as positively as possible, because we rarely know either."

Greg drew back in his chair and crossed his legs. Miss Huntley continued.

"How can you tell a kid like Georgie that his mother is always going to be an alcoholic, and that she doesn't want him."

"Alcoholic?"

"Didn't I tell you that?"

"No."

"Oh, I'm sorry. Saturday morning was so hurried; I just needed a home for him, fast."

"What's the story?"

"Well, several times the police found Georgie locked out of the house, skimpily dressed, while his mother was inside in a fit of intoxication. A neighbor would call the police each time."

"You mean he'd be out in the cold?"

"Yes, evidently, until the neighbor would see him. Then she would take him inside her house and call the police."

"That's incredible!"

"Let me backtrack a little. I was going to call you sometime this week and tell you this anyway. We haven't been able to contact Georgie's mother. We think she has skipped town, maybe gone back to her home in West Virginia. You see, they've only been in Indiana a few months."

"Why did they come here?"

"To find work, I guess. However, each time the police were called in, she made the statement that she needed to be by herself for awhile and needed the time alone. But the last time she got drunk and locked him outside, she told the police that Georgie was too much responsibility and that she didn't want him anymore. Her story didn't change even when she was sober. Anyway, the police took Georgie to juvenile detention. That's when we were called in to make him a ward of the court and to find him a foster home."

A feeling of horror shuddered through Greg's body! Imagine! Your own mother casting you away . . . maybe forever! Coming from a Christian home, Greg had experienced loving and caring parents. But what if you were not wanted? What must go through a child's mind? Greg remembered, as a child, worrying about the death of a parent, hoping that he would never be left alone. But for Georgie, it was a reality. To Georgie, it was as if his mother had died!

"Is there anything on his father's whereabouts?"

"No, nothing on his natural father. I don't think Georgie's mother even knows who he is. She's always living with a different man. In fact, that's probably why we can't find her presently. She's probably with a new one . . . somewhere. The West Virginia Department of Public Welfare informed us there was a man in the picture for awhile around the time Georgie was born. I guess they were all on welfare and food stamps together. She tried to get him to pay child support after he left her, but of course there was nothing legal to prove anything. Actually, there's no father listed on Georgie's birth certificate. My hunch is that she'll do anything to get money—other than honest work, that is."

"Wow," Greg stared in amazement at the floor, "what a story!"

"Yes, and the sad part is there are many stories like this one—some not as bad, some worse."

"So what can I tell him?" Greg looked at Miss Huntley hoping to receive some words of wisdom, some answers for Georgie, and some answers for himself.

"Really . . . it's up to you, Greg. The longer you have Georgie, the more you will know him better than anyone. Naturally, you don't want to upset him. I guess I would tell you to be honest with him and say to him whatever you feel you need to tell him."

Without upsetting him? No matter what—mothers are mothers! Special people. Why else would Georgie want to see someone who was a physical and mental mess, someone who abused him in so many ways? They were talking about Georgie's own flesh and blood!

Greg felt alone. Terribly alone. He thought it was not fair to him. He had not realized it would be this kind of responsibility. This wasn't in the package, was it?

At first, Greg could not work very well that afternoon. Every time he would start to get engrossed in something, he would be distracted thinking about Georgie. How was he going to tell him, and when? How would he bring it up to him that his mother was no longer in the area? Georgie would certainly sense that she did not care enough even to stick around where visitations might have been possible eventually.

Could he wait to tell Georgie until he asked about his mother again? Dare he do that? Was that fair to Georgie?

Questions cluttered Greg's mind, until he finally slammed the drawing pencil down on the table. Whom could he ask for help? He suddenly felt resentful that the welfare department had not helped him more. Wasn't that their job? Greg picked up the pencil and rolled it between his hands. He paced the floor for a few moments.

Maybe they had helped as much as they could. Besides,

it was his idea to be a foster parent. Greg recalled last Saturday when he and Georgie were in the grocery store. The clerk had thought he was Georgie's father! Greg quickly got up from his chair. He said out loud, "Well, if I want to be a father, I've got to **be** a father, not just act like a father when it makes me feel good or is convenient for me!" He felt a sudden relief from anxiety. "I needn't rely on any person, Lord. I've got You. Thank you for being with me."

Greg worked contentedly the rest of the day, not taking a single break. At two o'clock, chimes rang on the kitchen clock, and Greg went to the school to meet Georgie.

Standing inside the front door of the school, Georgie peered out as Greg drove into the parking lot. Greg could see Georgie's face perk up when he saw him. Greg smiled and motioned for Georgie to come out. He wished Georgie would have stayed in his classroom. It would have been nice to talk with Miss Stevenson again.

They got to the doctor's office a half hour early. Luckily, the waiting room had lots of toys. Georgie did not waste any time but began building bridges and arches with wooden blocks. He did, however, have a little problem sharing the treasures with an eager three-year-old, who wanted to play demolition instead of construction with Georgie's architectural designs.

"Georgie Stainer?" The receptionist called from her office booth. Greg raised his hand and then pointed to Georgie. "The doctor will see you now," she said politely.

Georgie looked pleased with himself that he did not have to put away the toys. He pointed out to Greg, "That little kid is still playing with them."

A nurse took them to a small, attractively decorated treatment room. The walls were ornamented with colorful pictures of animals, and several mobiles hung from the ceiling.

"My name is Mrs. Jackson," the nurse said pleasantly. She handed Georgie a white hospital gown. "Take off your shirt and jeans and slip this on. See . . .?" The nurse showed Georgie two long strings attached to the gown. "It ties in the back." Georgie did a double-take, first looking at Mrs. Jackson, then Greg, Mrs. Jackson, and back to Greg again. She smiled and started to the door. "The doctor will be with you in just a few minutes."

"I ain't takin' off **my** clothes!" Georgie abruptly announced as soon as the nurse closed the door. "**No way!**"

"You have to, Georgie. The doctor has to examine you, listen to your heartbeat."

"**No way!**" Georgie repeated and threw the gown on the examining table. "He'll jus' have to do it with my clothes **on** then!" Georgie plopped on a chair and folded his arms. His lower lip protruded and he frowned with great pleasure. He put Greg in mind of a Cigar Store Indian. He kidded Georgie about that, and Georgie turned the chair around to face the wall, still with his arms folded.

"Come on, Georgie. The doctor is a nice guy. He's not going to hurt you. He just has to make sure you're good 'n' healthy, that's all." Georgie grumbled and remained stubbornly facing the wall.

Sure is a feisty little fellow, thought Greg. God knows what he has been through as an abused child. He didn't seem shy about undressing for bed and baths at home. Maybe it was a natural modesty in him . . . or maybe with all the various men coming around his mother's house, it could be something different. He hoped not.

Mrs. Jackson came back into the room. "Say, you're not undressed yet. Here," she took a thermometer from a sterilized glass contained, "put this in your mouth; th-at's right, under the tongue now."

Georgie balanced the bitter-tasting instrument between his teeth and wrinkled his nose. "This thing tastes like medicine. How long does it haf' ta be in?"

"The longer you talk and don't keep it under your tongue, the longer it stays in," she scolded.

Georgie looked at Greg and rolled his eyes.

"Now, while that's in your mouth, I'll take your blood pressure." She looked at Georgie questioningly and raised her eyebrows. "It would be easier if you took off your shirt."

"Huh-uh," Georgie replied, shaking his head.

"Okay, then. Roll up your shirt sleeve." Nurse Jackson started helping him roll it up. "As far as it will go . . .tha-at's right." She strapped the mechanism to his arm and pumped the black ball for pressure.

Just then the door opened. A kindly looking gentleman in his mid-forties stood by the door smiling and glanced at the statistics the nurse had written on Georgie's chart. "Hi, I'm Doctor Hill." Greg stood to shake hands with the doctor and introduced himself. Then the doctor looked at Georgie. "And you must be Georgie," he said considerately.

Georgie immediately responded to Dr. Hill's gentle nature. He bashfully tipped his head and Nurse Jackson took the thermometer from his mouth. "Yep, I'm Georgie," he said shyly.

"Good. Now, let's see what your heart says . . ."

Georgie giggled. "I know what it says. Thump-thump, thump-thump."

"Oh, we have a promising young comedian in the crowd, go-od, good. Now, let's just slip off your shirt and find your heart."

"No!" Georgie snapped. Greg took hold of Georgie's arm and looked at him as a parent does when he wants his child to cooperate.

The doctor stood up straight. "Well, shucks," he whined as a child might, "I guess you won't be able to listen to your heartbeat then, huh?"

"Ya mean I can listen through that thing?" Georgie pointed to Dr. Hill's stethoscope.

"Uh-huh. But only if you promise to tell me what your heart sounds like again."

"Okay!" Georgie quickly peeled off his shirt, eager to hear his own heartbeat.

Georgie jumped when the doctor pressed the cold metal disc on his chest. Then Georgie tried it. He attached the earpieces and shouted as if he had on headphones. "See, I told ya!" He gestured with his arm. "It goes, thump-thump, thump-thump, thump-thump! Neat-o!"

Next, the doctor checked Georgie's reflexes with a rubber hammer. Georgie thought it was funny. He acted as if he had never experienced these things. Maybe he hadn't.

While the nurse checked Georgie's eyes, Dr. Hill told Greg that Georgie was in fair shape; maybe a bit small for his age because of evidence of slight malnutrition. "But nothing that a balanced diet and regular sleep wouldn't cure," he said.

The melting snow was a mess. It was good to be home again after running around in the sloppy slush half the day.

Greg relaxed in the living room after putting Georgie to bed. Another day! Such busy days, too. But he was getting used to it. He thought Georgie was happy— happy as a child could be without "natural" loving and caring parents.

Chapter 8

Soft music played from an FM radio in Greg's office.
The sun shone brightly from the east behind remnants
of winter's clouds, desperately trying to rid the ground of
snow, and to some avail; road conditions were becoming increasingly better, and the temperature was in the
middle forties.

The 10 a.m. munchies struck Greg as he put the finishing touches on a blueprint. He had already eaten breakfast with Georgie earlier that morning. How could he be
hungry again? Normally, he would not have eaten anything until the afternoon. And then it would have been
something light—soup or a sandwich. Maybe it was
good, thought Greg, a regular eating and sleeping routine.
Before he could get to the refrigerator, the telephone
rang.

"Hello."

"Hello, Greg? This is Theo."

"Theo, hi! How are you doin'?"

"Great. How are you doing, Daddy?" Theo snickered.

"How'd you know, Theo?"

"My mom said she saw you in church Sunday, and some other lady told her that you're a foster parent."

"My, news does travel fast," Greg laughed.

"Well, join the ranks, pal. Now you'll find out real fast what it's like to be a parent."

"That I'm doing." Greg stretched the long extension cord on the telephone so he could reach the refrigerator door. He tucked the receiver under his chin and poured a glass of milk.

"What I'm calling about is this. This is my weekend to have Karen, and I'm taking her to Indianapolis to show her around—maybe go to a museum and the zoo. We're leaving Friday evening and coming back Sunday. Since you have your foster son, I thought it would be fun if you guys went along."

"Sounds good to me. And I'm sure Georgie has never done anything like that before. He'll really enjoy it." Greg took a swallow of milk. "How old is Karen now?"

"She's seven."

"Georgie's six—almost seven."

"Great, they're about the same age. Listen . . . we'll pick you guys up around five Friday afternoon. It'll take us a few hours driving. Oh yeah, don't forget to pack bathing suits. I'll reserve a motel that has an indoor pool."

"Sounds like fun. It's been great talking to you, Theo. We'll see you Friday then."

Most of Greg's high school friends were married or had moved away. Theo was the only friend in the old gang still around town.

It was nice to have a friend like Theodore Collins. Not only was he a good friend and confidant, but an interesting person. He was exceptionally talented in sports, music, and art; and Greg remembered him as being very popular and active in high school. After high school, they had lost contact with each other. Theo was married the year after they graduated. And now he was a successful lawyer. Around the same time of Trudi's death, Greg had heard that Theo and Alice were divorced. Greg was shocked and saddened by that news and phoned Theo to talk. Their friendship was renewed after over eight years of hardly ever having the opportunity to socialize. Although their circumstances were different, with Theo's divorce and Trudi's death, they frequently shared their experiences with each other.

Greg saw the mail truck driving by and quickly ran outside to the mailbox. Even though the sun was shining, there was still a crispness in the air. Just another bill, thought Greg, as he glanced into the box and saw a letter inside.

The return address on the letter was "Gordon-Smyth Associates, Architects and Engineers, New York." Greg tore it open quickly. He recognized the name Gordon-Smyth. The architectural firm was one of the largest in New York City. Why were they writing to him?

Greg walked back to the house and read the letter quickly. "What? I can't believe it! Oh, wow! I just can't believe it!" Greg was so elated, he read the letter again, deliberately and slowly this time. He felt as though he were dreaming and needed to read it aloud to convince himself it was real:

Dear Mr. Larwell:

Gordon-Smyth Associates are continually seeking new, professional, expert talent. We are a rapidly growing firm, adding as many as five staff members each year.

Recently, my associate, Harriet Smyth, and I examined some blueprints you executed for Howell-Howell Associates, Louisville. We were impressed with your work and would like to meet you. We are extending an invitation to you to visit our facilities for three days, including an initial interview.

If you should decide to accept our invitation, please bring your portfolio and resume and be at our suites by Wednesday noon, April 6. Accommodations have been reserved for you at the Waldorf-Astoria. You are our guest and all expenses will be reimbursed.

Please call our offices collect by Monday, April 4, to confirm your visit. If April 6 is not convenient, you may call to arrange another date. If we do not hear from you, we will assume you are not interested. Sincerely yours,

Haysworth P. Gordon,
Gordon-Smyth Associates,
Architects and Engineers.

April sixth. That's next Wednesday! Greg fixed coffee and sat down at the kitchen table to contemplate the situation.

Imagine! New York City! He gathered in his mind all the drawings he would need to take with him to make up a portfolio. There was no question that he would go. An opportunity like this doesn't come up every day.

"Georgie!" Greg slouched down in the straight-back kitchen chair. He was so caught up in the excitement that he had forgotten about Georgie. "Georgie," he repeated. "What am I going to do with him while I'm gone?" Taking Georgie with him was out of the question. But he just couldn't pass this up; it was too big.

Greg returned to his office and tried to work. He had to laugh when he thought of his predicament. There **was** some humor in the whole thing. Here he was, twenty-eight years old, single, and worried about where he was going to find a baby-sitter for three days!

Just as he began an intricate segment of a drawing, the phone rang. "How's a guy supposed to get any work done around here when the phone's ringing off the hook?"

"Hello."

"Mr. Larwell?"

"Yes, this is he."

"Hi, this is Anne Stevenson, Georgie's teacher."

"Oh, yes! Hi." How odd that a teacher would be calling in the middle of a school day, thought Greg, unless . . . "Is everything okay? Is Georgie sick or something?"

"No, he's not sick. However, he did get into a fight a little bit ago at recess. His eye really got clobbered. The principal and I thought maybe you should take him to a doctor, just to check him out. Can you come to get him?"

"Of course. I'll be right there."

Georgie **was** feisty, but he did not seem the type to pick fights. If he did, thought Greg, it must have been something really upsetting. Poor little guy. He has had a lot happen to him in less than a week.

Georgie sat in the principal's office, leaning his head back and holding an ice pack on his left eye.

"Georgie? Let me see your eye. What's this all about?" Georgie slowly and painfully removed the ice pack. His eye and temple were puffy and red, soon to be black and blue.

"A real shiner, huh?" A tall black man dressed in a sporty three-piece suit stood behind Greg and Georgie. Greg's attention had been immediately focused on Georgie, so he hadn't noticed anyone else in the room. "Hi, I'm Mr. Reittor." He extended his hand to Greg. Greg was on his knees attending to Georgie and felt a little ridiculous shaking hands that way.

"Nice to meet you, Mr. Reittor. I'm Greg Larwell, Georgie's foster father. Sorry we have to meet under these circumstances . . . What happened here, anyway?" Just then Miss Stevenson entered the room.

"Hi, Mr. Larwell. Sorry to call you away from your work."

"What's this all about?"

Miss Stevenson smiled. She seemed to put people at ease in any situation. "We don't know; Georgie wouldn't say. He said he wanted you. That eye should be looked at anyway, so I called you."

Greg took Georgie's hand. "What happened? Who hit you in the eye? Do you want to tell me about it?"

Georgie puckered his mouth, and suddenly streams of tears rolled down his cheeks. He made a sudden motion, as if his left eye were hurting. But he kept on crying. Whatever was bothering him hurt more than the physical pain.

Miss Stevenson handed a Kleenex to Georgie. "Thank you," he said in a quivering voice. Greg held Georgie tightly and patted his back.

Soon the crying stopped, except for an occasional sniffle. "Are you ready to tell us now?" Greg asked.

"Who hit your eye, Georgie?" Miss Stevenson questioned in a soft whisper. She gently dabbed his tear-filled face with a Kleenex.

Greg nodded to Georgie to go ahead. "I . . . I can't tell ya."

Greg stood up. "Please, Georgie. Why did someone hit you?" Tears rolled down his face again as he mumbled something. Greg knelt beside Georgie. "We can't understand you, Georgie. What did you say it was?"

"I said, I can't tell ya with **him** in here." Georgie pointed his right index finger at Mr. Reittor.

"Georgie," Greg stammered, feeling a little embarrassed.

"He's the principal. Whatever you have to say, Mr. Reittor should hear it, too."

"Yeah, but he's black," Georgie said in an undertone. He was facing Greg, but it was loud enough for all to hear. "When he hears the bad name that kid called Henry, he'll get mad."

"You didn't say the bad word, Georgie. Mr. Reittor won't be mad at you."

Georgie looked up. Mr. Reittor smiled and gave Georgie a reassuring nod.

"Okay, then," Georgie sighed. He spoke in a low, whining tone. "Well, ya see, this big fourth-grader, I don't know his name, he started shoving Henry around an' calling him . . . nigger, an' stuff. So I went to help Henry, an' that kid called me a nigger lover. I told him he better watch his mouth . . ." Georgie started to sob. "An' then he said, you're jus' a stupid orphan. An' that's when I started to slug him!" Georgie quickly stopped crying. It was like he was suddenly aware that he was crying in front of all these people and he did not want to.

"We'll find out who the fourth-grader is, Mr. Larwell, and give him a good talking-to." Mr. Reittor thanked Greg for coming to school, and Greg told him Georgie would be in school the next day.

Dr. Hill was surprised to see Georgie back in his office so soon. He told Greg to keep an ice pack on Georgie's eye all evening, and if there were any signs of unusual drowsiness to call him at his home.

After supper the swelling in Georgie's eye had gone down considerably, but his disposition had also dropped. He seemed very depressed as he stared at a program on TV.

Greg lay down on the floor beside Georgie, with his hands propping up his head toward the TV. "What's wrong, Georgie-boy?"

"Nothin'," Georgie said glumly.

"Remember what I said a couple of days ago?" Georgie shook his head no. "I said if ever there is something bothering you, tell me about it and I'll try to help you."

"Promise ya'll help me?"

"I'll sure try, Georgie."

"Well, ya told me ya were goin' to see Janet 'bout seeing my mommy."

Greg knew what Georgie was getting at. He felt panicky. It was too soon. He wasn't prepared to answer. Georgie slowly pulled himself up and leaned against the chair. "Well, anyways, ya didn't tell me 'bout what Janet said." Georgie lowered his head and said pathetically, "My mommy don't want me . . . I know she don't. That kid at school was right . . ." Georgie's small body trembled and his voice cracked. "I **am** a orphan . . .''

Greg held Georgie's hand. There was complete silence between them. They lay side-by-side on the floor watching TV for a long time.

What if the job in New York developed into a reality? thought Greg. A guy has to think of himself . . . like his vocation . . . and his soul . . . But this little guy has a soul, too. Greg loosened Georgie's hand and stretched. He wouldn't worry about the job right now. Besides, they might not even offer him a position. He reminded himself to take one day at a time and trust.

Greg thought that Georgie really seemed to be sharp, right on top of things. Kids know when they're not loved or wanted. They're not dumb.

The silence was finally broken when Georgie asked if he could have cookies and milk for a snack. Greg thought Georgie must be feeling a little better.

In all the excitement of the day, Greg had forgotten to tell Georgie about the Indianapolis trip. It turned out to be a good way to cheer him up. Georgie went dancing and singing through the mobile home. Greg also hoped to fit in a visit with Doris and Randy, since they lived just outside of the Indianapolis city limits. They did not know about Georgie, so he decided he would not call them but make it a surprise visit.

"Do you want to say prayers tonight?" Greg asked as Georgie climbed into bed.

"No," Georgie replied bashfully.

"Okay, close your eyes."

"I would if I could," Georgie blurted, pointing to his black and blue eye. Greg and Georgie laughed.

"Dear Lord, thank you for this beautiful day. Forgive those who are unkind, and help us to forgive them. Thank you for fun things, like trips to Indianapolis. Bless us as we sleep and on the road tomorrow. Bless Georgie's mother and his friend, Jim. Amen."

"An God bless Miss Stevenson an' Henry. Amen." Georgie added quickly.

"And God bless Miss Stevenson and Henry," Greg said and smiled at Georgie. "Everything will be fine, Georgie. Love you."

"Love ya, too," Georgie said, hugging Greg.

Greg found a comfortable spot on the living room floor and watched TV. He stretched and yawned several times. How could he be so tired? The phone rang just as Greg started to doze.

"Hello."

"Hello, this is Anne Stevenson calling again."

"Oh, hi!" Greg felt a nice feeling come over him.

"I just called to ask about Georgie. Is his eye better?"

"Yes," Greg chuckled. "But it has turned all colors of the rainbow. It's not very pretty. It's really nice of you to call."

"I was concerned about him. All he wanted to do was help Henry and he ended up getting socked. The other thing I was wondering is if you and Georgie could come over for dinner next Friday night? I really admire you for taking on a foster child. I just thought you might enjoy a night out. You wouldn't even have to cook!"

"That sounds great, Miss Stevenson—"

"Please. Call me Anne. 'Miss Stevenson' sounds so formal."

"Okay, and please call me 'Greg.' About Friday, that sounds great, but I'm flying to New York next Wednesday morning and coming home Saturday morning—that is, if I find a baby-sitter." Boy! Did that ever sound like a hint, thought Greg. Nothing like sounding like a jerk!

"I'll take Georgie the three days you're gone," Anne quickly added. "I'd **love** it!"

"No, really. I didn't mean to sound like I was hinting."

"I didn't take it that way at all. I think it would be fun."

"Are you serious?"

Anne laughed. "Well, if **you** can do it, so can **I**."

"You're on! But I hope you know what you're getting into."

"Don't forget, I have kids around me day in and day out," Anne laughed. "I live at 557 Arthur Court. You can bring him over Tuesday evening if you want. That way you'll be free Wednesday morning."

"That would be great. Let's see, that's 557 Arthur Court, right?"

"Right. Have a good evening. Goodnight."

"Goodnight, Anne."

Chapter 9

Georgie charged out of the school bus into the house. He looked excited. His hair was blown in all directions from running, reminding Greg of last Saturday, the first time he saw Georgie. He had not seen Georgie so excited. Georgie squirmed and giggled with mysterious elation. "Guess what!"

"Goodness, you look happy—what?"

"Ya git three guesses!"

"Okay, eh . . . let's see. You got an 'A' today in school?"

"Nope!"

"You have a girlfriend?"

"No!" Georgie giggled.

"Okay, eh . . . you broke the world's record in high-jumping?"

Georgie laughed. "No, that ain't it neither. D'ya give up?"

"Guess so. I can't think of anything else."

Georgie stood straight up and looked as if he would burst with excitement. "I'm goin' ta stay with Miss

Stevenson when ya go away! But I didn't know ya was goin'."

"I haven't had time to tell you, Georgie."

"What ya goin' for?"

"Just business."

"D'ya have a suitcase I can use? I wan'ta start packin'."

Greg grinned. "Oh, not yet, Georgie. That's not 'til next Tuesday night. You'll have plenty of time to get ready. But speaking of getting ready and packing, we have to start getting ready to go to Indianapolis. They're picking us up in a couple hours."

Georgie clapped his hands and rushed to his bedroom. He busily took all his clothes from the drawer and dumped them on the bed. While Georgie was busy, Greg cut off an old pair of Georgie's jeans to use for swimming trunks. Later, Greg had to sort through Georgie's clothes and take out the amount he wanted to pack.

While fixing sandwiches for Georgie and himself, Greg began thinking about Gordon-Smyth. They had to be called no later than today if he was going for the interview. And he **was** going. Whether he got the job or not—a few days in New York City would be a nice experience.

After they ate the sandwiches, Greg called the Gordon-Smyth office and confirmed his visit with them the next week. Then he and Georgie played *Sorry* while they waited for Theo and Karen.

A horn sounded from a car parked outside the mobile home. It was Theo and Karen, right on time. Greg grabbed the large suitcase and gave a last-minute check to make sure everything was done—heat turned low, lights out, windows shut tightly.

Georgie watched from the front door as Karen got into the back seat of her dad's car. "Is that Karen?"

Greg quickly peered around the door as he checked the door lock. "Yep, that's her."

"Well, why is she gettin' in the back seat?"

"I guess because her dad told her to, so I can sit in the front seat and talk to him."

"**No way!**" Georgie scoffed. "I ain't sittin' in the back seat with no girl! **No way!**"

Greg turned and tightly held Georgie's shoulders. "Now just calm down, Georgie. I want to sit up front so I can talk to Theo. Besides, Karen won't bite!" Greg smiled and gently shook Georgie's arms.

"No!" Georgie shouted defiantly.

Greg could feel his face getting red. He knelt in front of Georgie. "Now look, I don't want **any** fuss!" Greg stood and gestured to leave. "There are some things in life you just have to do. And besides that, you're not going to get things by stomping around here and getting mad."

Georgie's eyes filled with tears. "I'm sorry," Greg said, lowering his voice. "But I don't like it when you shout and everything." The horn blew again. "They're waiting for us. Let's go." The tears stopped quickly. Greg thought it was because Georgie's left eye looked too sore to cry!

Introductions were made, and Georgie squirmed into a corner of the back seat. It wasn't fifteen miles later until Georgie and Karen were laughing and talking and playing some games Karen had brought with her. In fact, they were having so much fun it was hard for Greg and Theo to carry on a conversation.

After checking into the motel, the foursome headed for the indoor pool area. It was glass enclosed and there were tropical plants all the way around. A pool attendant informed them that cut-offs were not allowed as a substitute for a bathing suit. Greg and Georgie made a quick trip to a nearby variety store for what Georgie called a "real" swimming suit.

Everyone was getting hungry. Greg and Theo decided they would go out for a pizza after Georgie and Karen were done swimming.

It was good to talk with another adult. He and Theo sat at a round metal and glass-topped table beside the pool watching Georgie and Karen splash and jump in the water. They were the only people using the pool at that time. Georgie was having the time of his life. Such luxury he had never known. Greg bought four soft drinks from a machine and set them on the table.

Taking a sip of his drink, Theo teased, "So tell me, Greg—what have you been doing the last couple weeks besides cooking and working?"

"Not much." Greg shrugged his shoulders and laughed. "I **did** meet a nice girl the other day. I'd really like to take her out, but . . . I don't know."

"What do you mean?"

"It's stupid, but I just keep comparing every girl I meet with Trudi. I can't seem to get Trudi completely off my mind."

"That's not so bad," Theo empathized. "I wouldn't think much of you if you did!"

"But I feel—" Greg lowered his head to fight back the tears. "I feel like I'm betraying Trudi when I go out with other girls."

"Greg—I don't know how to tell you this . . . but I think you need to hear it." Theo's voice softened. "Trudi isn't coming back. Do you think Trudi would want you to remain single your entire life? I really doubt that. You can't dwell on her forever; you've got to remember the good times you had together and your love for each other. But leave it at that—you'll kill your mind if you don't. You know—I'll always love Alice too."

"Sorry, Greg. I sound like I'm preaching at you." Theo pounded his fist on the table and said kiddingly, "That's sermon number forty-three. Please deposit an additional quarter for sermon number forty-four!" Greg and Theo laughed. "But seriously, Greg—when Alice left me and ran off with that other guy, I thought everything between us had been going fine. She left without a minute's notice. Of course, I was shocked . . . it was like a death to me and all the struggles that follow. My world had caved in."

"But don't you hate that guy?" Greg interrupted, snapping at Theo in a fit of frustration. "Trudi's killer—that drunken idiot is alive and doing his thing and Trudi is six feet under!"

"She's with her Maker," Theo shot back.

Greg put his face in his hands and slowly shook his head back and forth. "I'm sorry, Theo. I didn't mean that. It's just that—I guess it's hard for me to love again when I hate so much. And it seems no matter how many times I ask God for peace and strength and forgiveness . . . well, I just fall again."

"But He always picks you up, doesn't He?" Theo smiled. "I mean, I hated too. But I learned hatred only made things worse for me and for everyone concerned. I had to think of Karen. I finally asked God to forgive me and asked Him for His guidance and help. I had to believe something, because at the time nothing seemed real." Theo lightly touched Greg's hand. "Have faith, Greg. Have faith that God has your life under control. Pick up the pieces and go from there. Just pray, pray, and pray."

"I've been trying to do that. And Georgie has really helped in the last couple weeks to make me think of someone besides myself."

"That's good," Theo quickly added. "Yet, Georgie can't fill the gap for Trudi. You're going to have to work that out within yourself, not just by keeping busy with Georgie. What if someday you're not busy again? No— you've got to sort it out in your mind and with God first."

Greg took another sip of pop. He acknowledged Theo's comments only by nodding his head.

"There I go again, Greg, preaching! Sorry, I don't mean to. It's only that I feel so much at peace and I'd like you to experience that peace too. The love of God—there's nothing like it. By the way, Greg, you never did tell me the name of that girl you met."

"Hey, Daddy, watch me dive!" shouted Georgie, distracting Greg and Theo from their conversation. His voice echoed throughout the huge room as he stood at the top of the ladder of the high dive.

"I'm watching," Greg yelled. He felt apprehensive about Georgie diving. However, the pool was not too deep and he was right there. He had been watching Georgie dog-paddling and thought he was fairly good at staying afloat.

Georgie started to run to the end of the board and then stopped at the very edge. He quickly walked back to the top of the ladder after seeing how far he would have to go down to the water.

"I don't think I'll dive, I'll jus' jump!" he called. At that, he darted off the edge of the board, making clownish gestures as he fell.

"He calls you 'Daddy'?" questioned Theo. "Won't that make it kind of rough when it comes time for him to leave?" Greg's eyes followed Georgie until he had safely dog-paddled to the side of the pool.

"Yeah, I guess so. But he doesn't really **have** a father. If he did, I would feel uncomfortable with him calling me that. I feel very fatherly; call it instinct or whatever. It gives me a close feeling towards Georgie, and I think it does Georgie too."

"If it has helped your relationship with each other, that's great," Theo commended.

"Well, the other thing is that it doesn't look as if he'll be leaving soon—at least that's what I gather from the welfare department. His mother doesn't want him and his relatives apparently don't want to be bothered with him either. Sad, huh?"

"Very sad. He seems like such a nice little guy, too. Would you consider adopting him if the opportunity came up?"

Adopt? Greg Larwell **adopt**? Never! That possibility had never crossed his mind.

"Oh . . . no," Greg said, smiling superficially, "I couldn't do that."

"Why not?" Theo questioned, becoming more and more interested.

"Well, I don't know." Greg stumbled for words. "I just wouldn't, that's all. I'd never thought about it."

Georgie climbed out of the pool, clutching his arms because of the cool air. He ran to the table, his wet feet making a patting sound on the cement floor. Greg held open a large beach towel as Georgie quickly cuddled his wet body into it. Karen followed, in turn, to Theo.

The children decided they had finished swimming and announced that they were very hungry. After Georgie and Karen got dressed, they all got into the car and drove a couple of miles to a small, quaint-looking Italian restaurant. It had attractive Mediterranean decor, the tables covered with red and white checked tablecloths, candles in the center.

Everyone had his own idea of what he wanted on the pizza. Finally, it was decided that each person could order his own nine-inch pizza with his choice of ingredients.

"Do you want to say the prayer, Georgie?" Greg asked when the pizzas arrived. Much to Greg's surprise, Georgie closed his eyes and prayed aloud for the first time.

"Dear God, thanks for the pizza. Amen."

"Thanks, Georgie," Theo said approvingly.

"Yes, thanks, Georgie," added Greg.

"Let's eat!" Karen piped in.

"Sure, everyone dig in," Theo invited.

After they returned to the motel room, Georgie and Karen changed to their pajamas and everyone played *Uno* until ten-thirty. Then it was "lights out" in anticipation of the next day.

Greg did not have any problems getting Georgie up in the morning. The day promised fun things to do, and Georgie was anxious to get started. After enjoying an eight o'clock breakfast in the motel's dining room, Greg and Theo decided the Children's Museum would be the first thing on the agenda. When they arrived, they discovered it would not be open until ten. Crown Hill Cemetery, being only a few miles away, was the likely substitute for spending some time until the museum opened. At the cemetery, they visited the grave of Hoosier poet James Whitcomb Riley. Other notables' graves they saw were Benjamin Harrison, the twenty-third president, and outlaw John Dillinger. Apparently, Georgie had seen a television show about John Dillinger. He recognized the name "Dillinger" and started ducking in and out behind the tombstones, acting out a bank robbery shootout.

The Children's Museum, the largest children's museum in the world, had many exhibits and other things to see. A spectacular toy train layout captivated Georgie and Karen for thirty minutes. The majority of the afternoon was spent at the museum, so there was not time to visit the Indianapolis Zoo or the Indianapolis Motor Speedway and Museum.

For Georgie, the highlight came that evening. Greg and Theo took the children to a Walt Disney movie.

Georgie said he had never been inside a movie theater. About eight o'clock, he started to get tired—until Greg bought a large box of buttered popcorn, another new experience for Georgie. Greg marveled at what people take for granted—simple things like a box of buttered popcorn or a Disney movie. But for Georgie, almost everything was a first. Greg knew that Georgie would always remember these treasured moments.

Waiting in line to get out of the crowded theater, Greg saw Georgie tap Karen on the shoulder. "D'ya have a mommy?" Georgie asked. Karen replied that she did. "Where is she then?" Georgie inquired.

"My mom and dad don't live together any more. I live with my mom most of the time and with my dad every other weekend."

"Ya mean they're divorced?" Karen nodded her head. Karen, obviously prompted by Theo not to talk about Georgie's past, remained silent. "Well, I got a mommy too, but I ain't living with her right now," Georgie rattled in a positive manner. "But I didn't have a daddy 'til now. Greg's my daddy now," he said, puffing his chest and grinning.

The next morning they attended a service at Christ Church Cathedral on Monument Circle. Greg explained to Georgie that the historic church was the oldest church in Indianapolis. That didn't seem to impress Georgie. However, Greg was taken by the beauty of the thirteenth-century reflection of Gothic architecture. He was in his element; this was his field.

After church, everyone went swimming before checkout time. Shortly, they were packed and headed for a visit with Doris and Randy before returning home.

Chapter 10

Doris and Randy were pleasantly surprised by their unexpected guests. The four adults visited around the kitchen table, while the children went to the family room of the tri-level suburban home.

It was always an uplifting experience to talk to Doris. She was positive and realistic in her approach to life. Her faith in Christ was practical—a daily walk. She turned to Him in every circumstance. Randy was a quiet sort of man. He usually listened intently when conversation among a group of people pointed a certain direction, and then added his comments which were well thought out and useful.

When the children were out of hearing distance,. Doris anxiously inquired about Georgie. "I'm surprised, Greg. Why didn't you call me and tell me about Georgie? I didn't even know you were thinking in that direction."

"I guess I didn't tell you that I applied for foster care several months ago," Greg interrupted.

"No, you didn't," Doris kidded Greg and looked at

Theo. "My little brother is always coming up with surprises. I think he's mellowing in his old age."

"Does he have parents and brothers and sisters?" Randy questioned.

"A mother is all. She's going through severe emotional problems. I don't know if he'll ever go back to her or not."

"What a shame," Doris said as she nodded her head sympathetically. "He seems like such a nice little guy, and so polite too."

"He is. I really haven't had any big problems. He seems very well adjusted for what he has been through. So, what d'ya think Sis, I mean about me having him?" Greg always looked to Doris for a type of parental approval. They had had a good relationship while growing up.

"Well, I think it's super, Greg. But can you handle it alone? I know there are times, many times, the kids get to me. I can always turn to Randy, and we work it out together."

"I suppose it is more difficult without a partner," Greg smiled. "But, since I'm not married, I just try to make the best of it."

"Speaking of women," Theo broke in the conversation. "You never told me who that girl was you met."

"Were we speaking of women?" Greg laughed. "Anyway, she is Georgie's first grade teacher. Her name is Anne Stevenson."

"I'm sure she's nice if my brother picked her," Doris said and poked Greg lightly on his arm.

"Let's not get carried away, folks. I just met her, and this whole group has me married." Everyone laughed. But she is nice, thought Greg. Very nice. In fact, Tuesday evening couldn't come fast enough for him. Taking Georgie to Anne's apartment would give him another chance to see her. He liked that. He had a good feeling about Anne.

The doorbell rang, giving Greg an opportunity to check on the children. When he returned, he was introduced to three couples with several children who were friends of Randy and Doris. The four couples met every Sunday afternoon in each other's homes for fellowship and prayer.

Randy and Doris insisted that they stay and join in. Greg felt they were imposing; but, after a little persuasion, he consented. "But tomorrow is a school day for the kids. We'll need to leave soon afterwards," he said—partly sincerely and partly because he had not been involved in any type of prayer group since Trudi's death. His faith had lessened and prayer groups were a thing for people who needed a crutch, as far as he was concerned.

The older kids who were visiting went to the family room to babysit for the smaller kids. The adults moved to the living room and set up chairs in a circle for their worship.

Randy led the group in an opening prayer and silence followed. Then one of the women started singing a song thanking Jesus. More prayers followed by different members. One man prayed for a healing of a broken marriage he knew of; another prayed for healing of mind and soul concerning the loss of a person in his family. Two others thanked God for things the Lord had done in their lives. Theo also praised God for the spiritual healing that had taken place in his life. There was more singing.

All this reminded Greg of the turmoil other people experience and that he was not the only one who had experienced loss and grief. The Spirit led Greg to pray.

"Heavenly Father, thank you for everyone's life and ministry. Thank you for the little person of whom I have been put in charge." Greg paused and fondly thought of Trudi. He swallowed hard and then proceeded. "And Lord, if it be your will, give me peace of mind concerning

Trudi." Greg stopped He couldn't go on without his voice shaking.

One hour later, Greg, Theo and the kids were in the car on their way home from Indianapolis. Georgie and Karen had fallen asleep in the back seat. Theo drove and seemed to be pondering the day's events.

Greg lay his head on the headrest and took a deep breath. He felt refreshed and eager to meet a new day. He sensed a different feeling within. Had the praying helped? Had he gained more faith? "Thank you, Jesus," he whispered. It was not a crutch, thought Greg. It was faith.

Chapter 11

"Hurry, Georgie! Bring that suitcase out here." Greg dried the last dish of the two-day stack. He wanted everything to be clean for their return home. "Hurry, Georgie," repeated Greg. "Don't you remember? Miss Stevenson called me during your recess today and invited us for dinner at six-thirty. It's almost that now!"

Georgie had been packing for a solid hour. He told Greg he did not want any help. Greg paced the floor. He was as nervous as a cat. First, he opened the refrigerator door, looked inside, and closed it. Then he straightened the tablecloth and rearranged the small appliances on the kitchen counter.

Greg made himself sit down and wait for Georgie. He felt ridiculous! He was acting like a high school boy going on his first date. Anne was such a gentle, personable individual. He hoped he wouldn't do or say anything awkward in front of her.

"Georgie! Are you about ready?"

"Coming," Georgie called as he dragged the suitcase

behind him, letting it drop on the kitchen floor in front of Greg.

"Are you all ready now? Have your toothbrush?"

"Yep! And I packed all by myself."

Greg checked the contents of the suitcase. "You did a super job, Georgie, but run and get a couple more pairs of underwear." Georgie had packed a few items he wouldn't need, but Greg let it pass. Georgie was so proud of himself.

"Hey, what's Miss Stevenson havin' for supper, anyways?"

"I don't know, Georgie," Greg chuckled. "I didn't ask her. It wouldn't be polite to ask. You just eat whatever a host or hostess prepares."

"Even if she gots peas?"

"Yes, Georgie. You've got to at least try everything."

"Yuk! I **hate** peas."

"Well, we don't know what she's going to have. Whatever it is, I don't want a fuss."

"Okay, but I don't like carrots, neither. Yuk!"

"Georgie—enough. You just do as I asked you to do without a fuss, and try everything, okay?"

"Okay, but can I tell ya somethin'?"

Greg looked at his watch. "It's time to go right now."

"But I jus' want to tell ya somethin'."

"Hurry."

Georgie giggled. "You like Miss Stevenson, **don't** ya?"

Greg smiled. "Yes, Georgie. I think Miss Stevenson is very nice."

Georgie picked up the suitcase. His eyes sparkled, looking up at Greg as he said tenderly, "She'd make a nice mommy, wouldn't she?"

"Yes," Greg murmured. That was all he could say to Georgie. Georgie was searching. The little guy had a certain look in his eyes, a haunting need for a normal

family. It must be terrible for him, thought Greg, not knowing what the future would hold.

The conversation made Greg edgy. He wanted to
quickly change the subject. It suddenly occurred to him
that Georgie was making a family of the two people he
was spending the most time with and growing to love
the most—his foster father and his school teacher.

Greg took the suitcase from Georgie. "Well," he said
brightly, "let's go."

Georgie ran to the car. Greg locked the front door of
the house and placed the suitcase in the back stall of
his MG. As Greg got into the car, Georgie held his hands
to the sides of his face. He looked away from Greg and
began to cry.

"Georgie?" There was no response. "Georgie?" Greg
gently loosened Georgie's hands from his red, tear-filled
face. "Georgie? Why are you crying? What's the matter?"
How could he change moods so fast? Greg momentarily
felt helpless.

"Please, Georgie. Can't you tell me what's wrong?"

Georgie sobbed almost to the point of hysteria. He
finally managed to cry out, "I miss m-my mom-my!"
Greg drew Georgie to him and held him tightly. Tears
welled up in Greg's eyes as he firmly shut them to keep
from crying.

"I know you do, Georgie. I know you do. Everything
will be all right, you'll see . . . You'll have fun staying at
Miss Stevenson's house this week."

Greg felt more helpless as a parent in this incident than
ever before. There were so many things to learn about
human need and compassion. It wasn't a completely
built-in sense. It would take time, time to understand
Georgie's whole makeup.

But love he could give him. That is what Georgie lacked
so intensely, needed so deeply. If only he wasn't going

to New York. Georgie needed him right now and **he** was going away. Could that have been part of the scene tonight? Of course, dummy, Greg scolded himself. Georgie was abandoned by his mother, and now **he** was abandoning him!

"Are you okay now?" asked Greg, as Georgie wiped the tears on his jacket sleeve. "I get back on Saturday. I'll have a special surprise for you."

"What is it?" Georgie sniffed.

"A surprise. You'll have to wait and see. Would you like me to call you from my hotel room—all the way from New York City?"

"Ye-ah." Georgie cracked a tiny grin. Those two promises seemed to help ease the situation for Georgie.

Anne served dinner as soon as Greg and Georgie arrived. They were fifteen minutes late, but she insisted she had just finished cooking. She had made spaghetti and meatballs, French bread, and salad. Georgie gave Greg a smile of relief when he found out there were no peas and carrots. For dessert, there was cherry pie topped with French vanilla ice cream.

Georgie made himself at home in front of Anne's color TV set while Greg and Anne drank coffee at the table. He explained the incident they went through before coming to her house.

"I thought I should fill you in as his guardian the next few days and because you're his teacher—just in case anything should come up. I hope nothing does." Greg finished the last of his coffee. "I really don't think anything will happen. Georgie was **real** excited about coming here."

"I'm not worried. You know—something I've noticed about Georgie is that sometimes he acts very grown-up and does very well in school. Then, other times, he's sort of babyish. But I can understand why. He has many things on his mind. Sometimes he is very agitated, almost anxious."

"Yes, I've noticed that at home sometimes, too."

Greg desperately searched in his mind for another topic of conversation. Georgie was about all they had in common. He didn't want to bore her like some parents do, when all they talk about is their kids.

"Have you always lived in this area?" Greg questioned. "Not to change the subject," he added quickly, "but I **had** been wondering."

"No, I'm originally from southern Indiana. After I graduated from college two years ago, this first grade position opened up. I applied for it and got it. So I moved here."

"I thought if you were from around here I would have met you sometime, somewhere. Do you like teaching first grade?"

"Oh, I love it. I did my student teaching in sixth grade, but I would never want to go back to that grade now that I've taught first. I love it. The kids are so neat at that age." Anne's eyes sparkled as she talked about her profession.

"And what about you, Greg, do you enjoy your work?"

"Do you know what I do?"

"Oh, yes," Anne grinned. "Don't forget, you have a first-grader—they like to talk. Georgie has told me all about the drawing table in your office—and the different pencils and pens and rulers you use. I assumed you were an architect, right?"

"Of sorts, yes," Greg said modestly. "I do free-lance work, independent contracts for firms all over the United States. It gets me around the country sometimes. In fact, that's why I'm going to New York this week. Only, this sounds like it could be a permanent position. I'm really not sure what it will open up."

"You mean it would mean moving there?"

Greg quickly put his finger to his lips, indicating the

need for lowered voices so Georgie would not hear.

"Oh, sorry," Anne whispered.

"That's okay." Greg tipped his head toward Georgie. "I just didn't want to upset him. He's got enough on his mind. Anyway, to answer your question," Greg softened his voice even more, "yes, I'd move to New York. I'm not counting my chickens before they hatch, but I'm sure it would be a decent salary with many benefits. But—there are so many pros and cons. It's an architect's dream to be singled out by a company like Gordon-Smyth." Greg checked the time on his watch.

"Would you like more coffee?" Anne got up and took the coffeepot from the counter.

"No, thank you. Everything was **so** delicious. Thanks for inviting us." Greg got up from his chair. "It's almost eight-thirty. I've really got to get some sleep tonight, and I still have to pack. My flight is at eight tomorrow morning—non-stop to Kennedy Airport."

"Well, I hope the best for you for a safe trip and a good interview. I'll be sure to pray for those things."

"Thank you, Anne. That really means something to me." Greg walked over to Georgie who was lying in front of the TV set. He had fallen asleep. Greg laughed to himself thinking of how Georgie loved color TV. It was his one chance to watch color, and he fell asleep.

"Georgie." Greg gently touched his arm and lightly smoothed his hand on Georgie's forehead. "Georgie, I'm going now." Georgie sleepily raised himself.

"You goin' ta be back Saturday?"

"Yes, Georgie. And I'll have that special surprise with me."

Georgie grinned lazily. "Can I tell ya somethin'?" he said quietly, looking at Anne as if he didn't want her to hear.

"What, Georgie?"

Georgie pulled on Greg's arm so he could whisper in his ear. "I love you, Daddy." Georgie hugged Greg tightly.

"I love you too, Georgie," Greg whispered. "See you Saturday." Greg turned to Anne. "And you be good for Miss Stevenson, won't you?"

"Yep," Georgie grinned. "You goin' ta be back Saturday, right?"

Greg smiled at Georgie reassuringly. "Right, Georgie."

Georgie went back to watching TV and Anne walked Greg to the door in the front hallway. "I don't know if you realize it, Greg, but that little boy is **captivated** with you. Did you see the way he looked at you? I don't think that anyone could convince him that you weren't his daddy!"

"I'm becoming attached to him—maybe too much so. There will come a time I suppose—he'll have to leave . . . Well, thanks so much for dinner. Oh, by the way, I'll call on Thursday evening to talk to you and Georgie. I promised him that. I'll be staying at the Waldorf-Astoria, so if you need to get in touch with me you will have to get the number from information and then leave a message with the hotel operator if I'm not in. Sorry I don't have the number."

"That's okay. There's no problem. And **please,** don't worry about Georgie."

"I know I won't. Not with you taking care of him." Greg stepped to the door and turned toward Anne.

"Have a safe trip, Greg."

"Thank you. And I'll see you on Saturday morning." Greg paused and looked directly at her. "Anne—I think you are a very nice person."

"Thank you, Greg," she said softly and smiled. "You are very nice, too."

Greg opened the door to leave and turned to face Anne once again. "Anne, would you mind if I held you?"

Anne held out her hands to Greg and they embraced. "Not if you don't mind if I hold you in return," she whispered. Just then Georgie rounded the corner into the hallway. They quickly separated and Anne blushed. Georgie smiled a wide smile and remained silent.

The evening air chilled Greg's body as he walked to his car. He buckled his seat belt and thought a few moments before starting the car's motor. He had a funny feeling leaving Anne and·Georgie. Suddenly, he felt very alone. It was the same sickening aloneness he had felt so many times since Trudi's death.

The engine roared to life as Greg switched on the ignition key. He glanced at Anne's apartment window and saw Georgie's head peeking through the living room draperies. Greg waved to him and Georgie readily returned the gesture.

There was a slight drizzle the next morning. It was just enough to make the roads slippery in spots. Greg parked his car in the airport parking garage and boarded his flight. Special airport trucks were heating the runway, trying to eliminate some areas of thin, slick ice. The flight was delayed for twenty minutes.

At Kennedy Airport, a Gordon-Smyth limousine was awaiting his arrival. It took him to the front entrance of a mammoth skyscraper where Gordon-Smyth leased the entire twenty-third floor of office suites.

With briefcase in hand, Greg boarded a large elevator. People jammed in tightly, momentarily causing Greg to forget his nervousness about meeting Mr. Gordon and Mrs. Smyth.

It was exactly twelve noon. Right on time. Greg laughed to himself. He was almost too prompt! An attractive receptionist greeted Greg as one might greet a foreign dignitary. She said Mr. Gordon and Mrs. Smyth were expecting him and took him to the presidential suite.

It was fabulous. A stone fireplace filled an entire wall. The other walls were lined with bookcases and expensive-looking paintings.

The co-presidents greeted him warmly as introductions were made. Mr. Gordon and Mrs. Smyth were very cordial but businesslike people.

That afternoon Greg was taken out to lunch and given a grand tour of the firm. He met many of the employees and was invited to examine a wealth of architectural instruments.

A Gordon-Smyth limousine was to take Greg to and from his hotel all week. He was overwhelmed by their hospitality.

At the hotel, a bellboy helped him to the fourteenth floor with his luggage. The room had a beautiful view of lighted skyscrapers.

After a snack, Greg took a long hot shower and put on his bathrobe. He spread out some drawings he had brought along and worked on them for an hour. Soon he was yawning and stretching.

Greg lay down on the king-sized bed, enjoying the softness of the sheets. He wondered how Georgie was getting along, and then recapped his conversation with Anne the night before. He somehow felt secure when he thought of her. He thought about how they had hugged each other. It was nice to be touched.

"Dear Father. Thank you for people, good people like Anne. And thank you for Georgie, too. Thank you for Jesus and the gift of eternal life. Help me to make important decisions in life, always keeping You at the head. Praise you, Father. Amen."

Chapter 12

The traffic below Greg's room flowed continually, as car horns blew a steady melody. Briefly forgetting where he was, Greg quickly glanced around the dark room. Moisture beaded on his forehead. The sheets were scattered in piles around the bed.

He had been dreaming. Such a stupid dream! Georgie had enlisted in the Navy. Greg was standing on a bridge waving good-bye to Georgie who was on a ship slowly sailing out to sea.

Greg chuckled to himself and checked the alarm clock on the bedside table. It was almost 4:00 a.m. Greg rolled over on his side, beginning to wake up. From the condition of the covers, Greg knew he had been tossing and turning in his sleep. He got up, rearranged the covers and wearily lay down.

Georgie popped into his mind again. Anne would probably go all out for him, fixing big breakfasts, taking time to talk, playing games. Greg smiled. "I miss the little guy."

What will happen to Georgie? His mother and relatives don't want him. Maybe he **should** check with the welfare department about adoption . . . just to see. Theo had seemed so positive about it.

Greg sat up in bed and turned on the bed lamp. Would the department allow a single man to adopt? Why not? That did not seem any more unusual than being a single foster parent. The light from the lamp glared into Greg's eyes. He switched it off and plopped back in bed. What was he saying? Georgie had a **mother.** Even though she **was** unfit, someday she might be able to get him back.

But he loved Georgie. What right did **she** have, a **drunk,** toying with someone's life! Greg thought bitterly of how Trudi was killed because of someone's drunkenness.

"Forgive me, Lord; the woman obviously has problems and can't help herself. But—think of the trauma she is putting her little boy through . . . is that **right?** Let Your grace be sufficient to me, Lord."

"Sleep," Greg muttered. "I must get to sleep. I'm going to have a full day tomorrow." He pulled the sheet to his waist and sighed deeply. "But I **am** going to check with Janet Huntley, just to find out the possibilities."

At 8:00 a.m. Greg was sitting across the desk from Mr. Gordon and Mrs. Smyth. The interview had begun. Two board members were also present.

"Mr. Larwell," Mr. Gordon began, "I'd like to get right to the point." Mr. Gordon looked at the other people present. "We at Gordon-Smyth are impressed with your portfolio, your credentials, and your references. We like you! Three newly created positions will be filled with persons who will be working exclusively from our offices here. Free-lance contract work is not allowed. However, if we decide to hire you out of the thirty-five individuals we will have interviewed, we are prepared to offer you almost double what you now earn."

"Mr. Larwell," Mrs. Smyth interrupted. "We are very impressed with you. We would consider you an asset and a fine addition to our staff. You are professional, sincere—and everything we look for at Gordon-Smyth. For years our reputation has been one of excellence. Should we decide to hire you, and you decide to accept, you would begin next January first. That is also when our fiscal year begins." Mrs. Smyth smiled. "Hopefully, that would give you plenty of time to decide on the position, should it be offered to you, and also to complete any individual contracts on which you might be working."

Mr. Gordon stood and said in a concluding voice, "We are prepared to make a final decision by August first. Would you be prepared to give us your final word by mid-August if a contract is offered to you?"

"Yes, thank you," is all Greg could say. The meeting was promptly adjourned, as the executives had a conference to attend. Greg was free to come and go as he pleased for the remainder of that day and the following one.

At noon Greg decided to go sightseeing for a couple of hours and also to buy Georgie a gift as he had promised. He remembered Georgie had wanted a football and football jersey. Greg bought the two items at Macy's.

That evening, after dinner at one of the hotel's dining rooms, Greg returned to his room. Instead of working, he decided to take advantage of his "vacation," and read the newspapers, snack on cheese and crackers, watch TV, and generally relax, which he hadn't had much time for lately.

At eight-thirty, Greg dialed the hotel operator to place the long distance call to Indiana.

"Hello. This is Anne Stevenson."

"Hi, Anne."

"Greg! How is everything going?"

"Just fine. I'm anxious to tell you all about it when I get home. How's everything going there?"

"Fine. I just gave Georgie a bowl of ice cream and some pretzels for a bedtime snack."

"Oh, before I forget it, let me give you my phone number. Got a pencil?"

"Yes, go ahead."

"Area code two-one-two, five-five-five, seventy-two hundred. Got it?"

"Yes, and I think there is someone here who wants to talk to you." Ann giggled. "It's a little person standing in front of me with chocolate ice cream on his face." Anne handed the receiver to an eager Georgie.

"Hello, Daddy?"

"Hi, Georgie. You having a good time?"

"Yeah."

"Is school going all right?"

"Yeah, an' ya know what?"

"What?"

"I told Henry that I was stayin' with Miss Stevenson for three days, and he don't believe me, so guess what?"

Greg laughed. "What, Georgie?"

"So Miss Stevenson invited Henry to her place after school tomorrow for brownies and milk. Then we're goin' ta go swimmin' at the indoor pool at the high school. Neat, huh?"

"Sounds really neat, Georgie. It's very nice of Miss Stevenson to do that. Now you be good—put Miss Stevenson back on again, please. I love you. I'll see you on Saturday."

"Okay, an' I love you too," Georgie replied cheerfully. "Hey, Miss Stevenson, he wants ta talk ta you again."

"Hello?"

"Hello again, Anne. Georgie said you are going swimming, and his swimming suit is at my place."

"That's okay. They always have a box of lost-and-found swimming suits at the pool. He can use one of those."

"Good. Well—thanks again for keeping Georgie. It's comforting knowing that he's there, and it's probably just what he needed—to stay with someone like you."

"He misses his daddy, too. You're the main topic of conversation!"

"Well—have fun at the pool tomorrow. I'll see you Saturday."

" 'Bye Greg, and the Lord be with you."

"And with you, Anne."

Greg spent all day Friday at the Gordon-Smyth firm talking to employees and observing their work and procedures. The more he saw of the firm, the more he liked it.

Saturday was a beautiful day. On the flight home, thousands of feet above the earth's surface, the clouds and mountains painted a gorgeous picture. Greg could tell when they were getting into western Ohio and Indiana. The mountains became hills and the roads straightened.

On the ground, the jet taxied toward its resting place. Greg looked out the port window by his seat and saw two familiar faces at the entrance gate. It was Anne and Georgie. They had come to meet him.

The plane stopped, and the engines were turned off, creating a high-pitched whirring and whining sound. Greg felt as though he was meeting his **family** as he hurried down the ramp.

Excitedly, Georgie ran to meet Greg. Georgie plunged into his arms and then Greg swung him around. He **was** his son! He could **never** give up Georgie.

Greg extended his hand to Anne and kissed her on the cheek. While they sat down to wait for his luggage, everyone exchanged their week's experiences. Greg used discretion in telling Anne about his interview, because of Georgie's presence.

Greg gave Georgie the presents he had brought from New York and Georgie changed into his jersey right in the lobby. He grinned at Greg. The footfall was exactly the one he wanted.

After Greg claimed his luggage, they went to a restaurant at the airport for lunch. The waitress seated them at a comfortable, cushioned booth. It was good to be back home.

"Georgie and I just thought it would be nice to have a welcoming party for you when you got off the plane. I hope you don't mind."

"Mind? It's the highlight of my week—and I mean that."

"I thought you'd be tired, so we brought Georgie's suitcase along so you won't have to make a stop at my place on your way home."

Greg smiled in unbelief. "Anne, you think of everything."

"Look, Daddy." Georgie unfolded a large map of the United States. "Here's Indiana—that's where we live ya know. And here's New York—that's where you was. Miss Stevenson showed it to me."

"And another thing," Georgie continued busily, "Miss Stevenson taught me a song." Georgie folded his map neatly and sat straight up in his seat. He had been talking rather loudly because of his excitement. When he started singing, his voice turned into a soft, sweet, angelic sound which was very much in tune. "Jesus loves me, this I know—for the Bible tells me so—little ones to Him belong—they are weak but He is strong. Yes, Jesus loves me—yes, Jesus loves me—yes, Jesus loves me—the Bible tells me so." The difference between Georgie singing in church every Sunday and now was that he knew the words. His voice was beautiful.

Georgie grinned bashfully at Greg and Anne. "That was beautiful, Georgie. Thank you. And thank you, Anne, for teaching it to him."

Things quieted down after the food arrived at their table. As Greg ate, he thought of Anne and Georgie. Two people he had known for a very short time had become the two most important people in his life—practically overnight.

Chapter 13

April showers descended during the remainder of the weekend and all day Monday. Dampness made it necessary to wear jackets and sweaters. Tuesday the weather cleared to a beautiful spring day with the temperature in the high sixties.

Greg worked steadily in his office. But Gordon-Smyth lingered in his mind as he tried to be creative in his drawing. Finally, at noon he decided a break would help clear his thoughts.

Driving into town for a cup of coffee would be relaxing, thought Greg—somewhere with **people** around! Sometimes just being with people, sharing conversation, talking about the weather which merited mentioning, would benefit his work. Now that he had Georgie, being in the company of adults once in awhile was more important than ever.

After several cups of coffee, Greg drove to a florist shop and ordered one dozen red roses for Anne, a thank-you gift for taking care of Georgie. He had them delivered to the school.

The temperature dipped into the forties that evening, but it was pleasant. After supper, Greg and Georgie took a casual walk around the mobile home court. Greg introduced Georgie to a few neighbors who were doing some spring lawn work. As they walked, Georgie remarked several times that a bicycle would be nice to have. He had never owned a bike.

"As soon as I can afford it, Georgie, we'll talk about it."

"For my birthday?" Georgie asked hopefully. "Ya know it's in July, don't ya?"

"Yes, Georgie, July second," Greg smiled.

"Well, do ya think you could 'ford one then—for my birthday?"

"We'll see, Georgie. I'd like to see you have a bike, too. But right now, we'll just have to wait and see. I've got some heavy bills coming up in the next couple months."

The welfare department appropriated a sum of money each month for Georgie. It barely covered his food and clothing expenses. Greg would have to purchase a bicycle out of his own money. He did not believe in apologizing to Georgie when money was involved. Even though Georgie was only six, Greg thought he should learn the value of money, that you could not always have something when you wanted it.

That evening Greg and Georgie ate whole-wheat toast with grape jelly, and shared a grapefruit, sprinkled with sugar, for a bedtime snack. Greg tucked Georgie into bed and they said their bedtime prayers together. Walking into his office, Greg switched on the fluorescent light over the drafting table. He still felt alert and decided to work a couple more hours.

At ten o'clock, Greg heard someone at the front door.

The noise he heard wasn't someone knocking but **opening** the door.

Theo! thought Greg. Funny, he hadn't heard a car drive up. Greg quickly laid his pencil on the table and started for the front door.

Startled by the presence of an unfamiliar woman standing in his doorway, Greg stopped cold in his tracks.

"Who are **you**?" Greg said with some alarm. "What do you want?"

The smell of alcohol filtered across the room toward Greg, as she slammed the door behind her and staggered forward a few steps.

"As if **you** didn't **know**!" she roared violently, spit drooling from her mouth to her chin. She swayed closer to Greg.

Greg stepped back. "No I **don't** know! Who are you **anyway**? What do you **want**?"

"Is your name Greg Larr-ell?" she sneered.

"Listen. I'm calling the police if you don't get out of here!"

"Hey, buster! I asked you a question—is your name Greg Larr-ell?"

Suddenly it dawned on Greg. Georgie's mother! What did she want? Why was she here? "Yes," Greg stammered, trying to calm down. "May I help you?"

"Don't give me that high falutin' psychiatrist 'may-I-help-you' bit!" the woman shouted, mocking Greg's question. "Yes! You can help me! Get Georgie!"

"I'm **sorry**. You're going to have to leave **now**! Or I'll call the police." Greg reached for the kitchen wall telephone and had started to dial when Georgie's mother clumsily struck it out of his hand. Greg could not believe what was happening. He would need to physically show her out of the house.

Just then, Georgie appeared in the hallway leading

from his. bedroom. "Mom-my!" His eyes were heavy from sleeping, yet there was also a horrified look in them. "What are ya doin' here—what's goin' on?" Georgie looked at Greg, his mother, and the telephone receiver dangling by its cord on the floor. "Why are ya fighting?" he whined.

"Shut up and come here, ya little brat! You're always askin' too many stupid questions. Get your coat and let's go."

Before Georgie could move, Greg spoke up. "Now listen here! You're not only breaking the law by barging into my home, but seeking out and trying to take Georgie is a direct violation of the court—"

"There ya go again, big college man, talkin' big. Well, I ain't talking no more, clown! Come on, Georgie!" She grabbed for Georgie who was now standing behind Greg, frightened and crying.

Greg snatched her wrist and tightly gripped the artery, preventing her from moving forward or backward. "You're not taking him anywhere! Georgie," Greg ordered, "dial the operator." Georgie looked at Greg. He looked as if he did not know where his loyalty should be. Then, reluctantly, he picked up the receiver.

"Ya goin' ta call the police?" Georgie whimpered as if his mother were a common intruder.

"Ya goin' ta call the police!" she mimicked and struggled to loosen her arm. Greg tightened his grip. "Ya little heathen!" she screamed. "Ya'd sell your own mother! You always **were** a little creep. Go 'head! **Dial** the operator! I don't want your little butt around me anyways!"

"Dial, Georgie," Greg ordered calmly, taking the receiver with his chin from Georgie. "Thank you, Georgie. Now please go to your room and close the door." Georgie edged to his door, now looking more concerned for Greg than his mother. Greg could hear Georgie in the bedroom crying. The police arrived ten minutes later. By then Georgie's mother had calmed down and sat silently in a drunken stupor.

As the police took her away, Georgie came running out to Greg, not saying a word. He clamped Greg's arm and they went to sit on the couch. Georgie just sat there staring, every once in awhile breaking into a muffled cry.

Greg remained silent. What was there to say? Somehow, thought Greg, Georgie realized that he would never again be with his mother, that he could sense the doubtfulness of a reconciliation.

Greg rocked Georgie and comforted him until finally Georgie lay in his arms, asleep. Greg carried him to his bedroom and carefully put him down. He tucked the covers securely around the little boy.

Georgie's face was streaked with dried tears. Greg wet a washcloth with lukewarm water and gently wiped Georgie's face. Georgie flinched and opened his eyes. Seeing that it was Greg, he smiled and sleepily closed them again.

Greg poured a glass of milk. He needed to calm down. He reenacted the incident over and over. It seemed like a dream to him. He was more shaken now than when it actually happened.

"I've got to talk to someone." Greg fidgeted. "I'll go bananas if I don't." It was past eleven o'clock. Hoping that Anne would still be awake, Greg hurriedly dialed her number.

"Poor Georgie!" Anne responded after Greg recounted the experience. "And **you**, Greg. I'm really concerned and sorry you had to go through an experience like that. Do you want me to come over to talk? I'll be glad to."

"No . . . That's really kind of you to offer, but I'll be all right. I already feel better just telling you this much."

"What did Janet Huntley say?"

"I didn't contact her."

"Oh, Greg. You should call her now!"

"Do you think so?"

"Most definitely. You should have called her right after the police left."

"Yes, I guess you're right. That never crossed my mind—it all happened so fast. I guess I was too shaken up to think about it earlier. But it's kind of late now."

"If I were **you**, I would call her immediately."

"Okay, and I'll get back to you tomorrow on any further developments. Thanks a million for being there when I needed you."

Greg called Janet Huntley and described the incident. She had been sleeping and sounded groggy. She did not seem to be too surprised; Greg thought she was probably used to that kind of thing.

"Oh, one more thing," asked Greg. "Even before this happened, I was going to call you. Now, this seems to be an appropriate time." Greg switched the receiver to his other ear. "Or are you too tired to talk?"

"No, that's all right. Go ahead."

"What are the chances of **me** adopting, I mean in general . . . no . . . I mean of adopting Georgie? Does this 'mother scene' change anything, as far as Georgie's status?"

"It certainly doesn't help her chances any. And from the sound of the way she talks to Georgie, what **she** misses is verbally abusing him—among other things. As far as adopting goes, we'll just have to wait and see what happens in the mother's case. She could be proven **totally** unfit, and Georgie could be made adoptive."

"But, what about me? I mean, being single? Does that hurt my chances?"

"Not particularly. It depends who the hearing judge is and other circumstances. It used to be harder for a single person to adopt, but the law doesn't require that there be two parents. Besides, the other natural parent hasn't been established, and the relatives don't want him. If the mother would be proven unfit, there wouldn't be any other hassle.''

"So there's a chance!" Greg anxiously paced the kitchen floor, dragging the telephone with him.

"Yes, a chance. But don't get your hopes up too high. There's an equal chance you **couldn't** adopt. The thing you **do** have in your favor, if adoption should come up, is that Georgie is apparently happy with you and he's six, going on seven years old."

"What do you mean?"

"When children are past infancy, people aren't as ready to adopt them. To put it crassly, they lose their market value."

"Oh, I see. Well, you'll be in touch then on further developments?"

"Yes, I'll call you. And—sorry about all the trouble. I don't know **how** she got your name and address! Being a foster parent, you put yourself in a position for trouble in some cases. Either the parents or the kids!"

"Yes, somehow you hope everything will be normal and 'la-de-da.' But realistically, the fact that a kid is a foster child says that things aren't normal."

Miss Huntley giggled. "How true. You sould like you're catching on fast. It doesn't take long when you have foster children. Well, Greg, all I can tell you is to let it ride for a few weeks. It's a waiting game. You'll just have to be patient."

"Okay. Thanks, Miss Huntley. Goodnight."

"Goodnight."

Greg lay down on his bed. All the thinking and talking about adopting Georgie was scary. When he applied for a foster child, he never dreamed it would be like this, or come to this! How confusing. And the New York possibility only complicated matters more. He needed to think. There were so many things to think about. Greg turned the stereo on softly and slid under the bed covers.

Georgie's spring vacation from school was coming up next week. Georgie needed a change of atmosphere and so did he. Maybe he could rent Theo's vacation lake cabin in upper Michigan for a few days. Yes—that sounded good! He and Georgie could fish and just relax.

Chapter 14

Theo had been very accommodating. Cookware, dishes, silverware, bed sheets, and pre-cut wood for the fireplace . . . everything Greg and Georgie needed was in or around the cabin.

The last twenty miles of the drive had been beautiful. There was nothing but pine trees, highway, and an occasional deer darting along—pure paradise.

The upper Michigan temperature was much cooler than in Indiana, especially the nights. When Greg and Georgie arrived, it was dark. They made themselves at home by fixing a warm fire. Two overstuffed chairs by the fireplace were conducive for Greg to read a novel and Georgie to color in his coloring book. No TV, no telephone, no drafting table. Just peace and quiet.

Sunday morning was a sight to behold. As Greg and Georgie opened the front door, they viewed a beautiful lake edged with pine trees and ringed with lily pads. Just a few cabins spotted the densely wooded shore. They were literally out in the middle of a forest.

While their breakfast of fried potatoes and ham cooked on an open fire, Greg and Georgie read a short devotion on the small pier near the front door of the cabin. The birds chirped sweetly and the morning sun rose across the lake, causing the water to appear as glittering crystals.

Greg fixed eggs after the potatoes and ham were cooked. Then they browned bread over the fire for toast. Greg watched Georgie as they ate. He thought Georgie was much more calm. It was a good idea to take the week off from work. He also thought Georgie had learned better eating habits, compared to when he first came to live with him.

Greg had not fished in years, and the only fishing Georgie said he had done was with his friend Jim. Novices or not, the pair shoved off in Theo's little rowboat as soon as breakfast was finished.

"Look how that little worm wiggles and squirms when I stab him with this hook!" Georgie yelled.

"Ssssh. You'll scare the fish away, Georgie."

Georgie whispered, "But look how he squirms!"

Greg chuckled. "You'd squirm too if someone were poking you with a hook."

Georgie threw in his hook and line. Immediately the bobber went under the water. Looking like a pro, Georgie yanked his pole. "I got one! I got one!" Georgie sang out.

Greg got the fish net and scooped the fish out of the water. Sure enough, Georgie pulled in the first fish of the day, a nice pan-cooking-size bluegill.

That was the first of many fish that day. Their only break was to eat a sandwich at noon. Many of the fish were thrown back, but not because of being too small; there were too many for them to eat.

That evening Greg and Georgie ate fried fish until their stomachs could hold no more. After the dishes were washed, they sat on the front steps. Greg played some folk songs on a guitar Theo kept in the cabin.

"That's a sad song," Georgie sighed after Greg had sung "Blowin' In The Wind." Georgie leaned back on his elbows and stared at the sky. "Look at them stars; ain't they purdy?"

"Yes, they are," Greg said quietly.

"God lives in the sky, don't He?" Greg nodded thoughtfully. "There's no trouble up there neither. That's what I heard that preacher on TV say. Everybody's nice to everybody else, and no one yells at no one, and no one's sad."

"That's right, Georgie," Greg replied reassuringly.

"Everybody dies, don't they, Daddy?"

"Yes, Georgie. At one time or another."

Georgie stared for several minutes. Finally he said softly, his voice slightly shaking, "I wish I could be up there," Georgie pointed his finger at the sky, "where nobody would yell or ya wouldn't hav' ta be sad."

Greg turned Georgie so he was looking directly at him. He thought Georgie's assumption had sounded too final, so desperate for a six-year-old boy!

"Are you sad right now, Georgie?"

"Kind of."

"But you know that I care for you, don't you, Georgie?"

"Yeah . . . I know."

"You don't have to be sad or afraid—I'll take care of you. No one will hurt you." Greg's voice brightened. "And God loves you very much too, Georgie. He has many things planned for you on this earth."

"He does?"

"Yep."

"What did He plan for me?" Georgie innocently questioned.

"Only He knows that. But He definitely has something planned for you. Did you know that God knows you better than you know yourself? Why—He even knows how many hairs you have on your head!"

"He does?" Georgie quickly reached for the top of his head.

"Yep, He does."

"Wow." Georgie said with amazement. "Can I ask ya somethin'?"

"Ask away, Georgie."

"Well—I was jus' wonderin' . . . are ya goin' ta keep me at your house?"

Greg had not anticipated that question, at least not yet; although, knowing Georgie's keenness, he should have realized it would come. How should he answer? He didn't know himself what would happen. If Georgie would want to stay and somehow it didn't work out that he could—he didn't want to get Georgie's hopes built up.

"Do you like it, staying with me?" Greg asked.

"Yeah." Georgie slowly nodded his head.

"Good . . . I'm glad. I like your staying with me, too." Greg hated not letting Georgie know one way or the other what would happen to him. But he couldn't afford to fill him with too much hope, not yet. Not until things were more certain.

"We'd better get inside, Georgie. It's getting too cool out here." Greg took the guitar and they went indoors.

Greg stirred the fire with the poker and then put Georgie to bed. He relaxed while reading by the light of the fire. What serenity, thought Greg. A peaceful flickering fire, a good novel—what more could he ask for? . . . Maybe Anne?

Greg closed the book and gazed into the fire. Sometimes he was surprised by his own thoughts. Could he be missing Anne? Really missing her?

Greg shifted positions in the chair and stretched out his legs closer to the fire. At that moment, he wished with all his heart that he could tell Anne about his feelings for her. But—what about **her** feelings? What if she didn't feel the same way? He couldn't afford to be "shot down." That was selfish, but there were too many feelings of being left alone since Trudi's death. He was lonely. But could he get involved again? Being lonely, alone, was one thing. But being lonely and wanting someone and not being able to have her was another.

Suddenly Greg thought of Georgie, and how Georgie's situation with his mother corresponded with his missing Trudi. Neither could have what was not there. Theo had said to pick up the pieces and go from there . . .

"Have faith, you doubter. I've got to have a more constant faith," Greg whispered. "My shepherd will supply my need. Certainly He will. Even though it might not be what 'Greg' wants. He will supply my needs. Look at Georgie—that certainly has supplied a need. Many needs. What do You want me to do, Lord?"

And then there was the matter of Gordon-Smyth, thought Greg. Mr. Gordon and Mrs. Smyth had sounded very positive. Mr. Gordon said there were thirty-five people interviewed and only three would be chosen out of that number. That was a pretty big 'if.' And there were many pros and cons. Moving away from a secure small town atmosphere to New York City could be a real cultural shock. Maybe the money would compensate for that. On the other hand—giving up the freedom of being self-employed could also be a drag—especially for someone not used to several people giving him orders. He would just have to wait, have faith, and pray.

The next day, Greg and Georgie drove to a small town about twenty-five miles from the cabin to get some supplies. They drank a soda in a quaint, turn-of-the century drugstore and then bought some fresh food and staples to take back to the cabin.

The vacation had been good for Greg and Georgie. And the weeks that followed were busy for Greg, working and going to Georgie's final school programs. He had seen Anne only a few times socially and at school functions.

It was on a Tuesday, the week before school was out, that Georgie came home complaining of an itching back. Greg lifted Georgie's T-shirt and saw two water blisters. They were rather large and had a reddish cast on the edges. Georgie's warm forehead indicated that he had a slight fever.

Greg recalled having chicken pox at seven years of age. He called Anne to get her opinion.

"There was a boy in class—Freddy. He came down with the chicken pox about two and a half weeks ago," Anne confirmed. "That's about the right amount of time from when you contact it until you show signs."

"Oh great," Greg scoffed. "Oh well, I guess that's how it goes. Anyway, I'm glad we know what it is. I thought if anyone ran into these situations, a teacher would." Greg laughed.

"You should probably get some lotion from your doctor and give him baking soda baths."

"Okay."

"Oh, and another thing," said Anne. "You **do** know that when the sores start scabbing over, he will no longer be contagious?"

"No, I didn't know that. Thanks." Greg paused. "Anne, sometime I'd like to be with you . . . go out somewhere, just you and I."

"That would be nice," Anne said softly.

"I've been wanting to do that more often, but it always seems that something comes up—now chicken pox!"

"Well, I'll really look forward to it, Greg. Every time we're together, I enjoy your company."

Could he really be hearing her right? He had hoped so much she felt the same way.

Chapter 15

The second day of chicken pox was worse than the first. Georgie had aroused at five a.m. itching and scratching, nursing a runny nose, and his temperature had risen. Later in the morning Greg called Dr. Hill who prescribed a lotion and baking soda baths!

Greg called Anne at the school and asked if she would pick up some lotion at the drugstore after school.

By noon, Georgie had ten big spots on his back, but none as big as the first two.

"Do you want a little tomato soup, Georgie?"

"I don't know," Georgie whined. "I've gots the running vowels."

"The what . . . ?"

"The running vowels, ya know."

"The running vowels . . . ?" Greg repeated to himself. "The running—oh! You mean bowels!" Greg roared with laughter. But seeing that Georgie looked embarrassed, he stopped laughing and tried to confine it to a smile.

"It's bowels, Georgie, not vowels," Greg snickered.

"You should eat something. Do you want to try a little soup?"

"Okay, I'll try some."

Soon after school, Anne arrived with the lotion. She also bought Georgie a coloring book and some Sprite.

Georgie was now complaining that his head itched. Greg could tell that Georgie felt miserable. It was hard for him to follow Greg's orders not to scratch. However, Anne's gifts helped some, as Georgie willingly went to his room to color and drink his Sprite.

Greg confided to Anne that he felt antsy not being able to get out of the house. "It's difficult meeting Georgie's constant demands. He will ask for one thing after another . . . and always just when I've finished doing something else for him and have sat down."

"It's hard for a little boy to be confined like this," Anne said sympathetically.

"Yeah, I know. I didn't mean to be hard on him. But I've been up since five o'clock with hardly a break from him. I certainly didn't get any of **my** work done to speak of." Greg looked toward the hallway and spoke softly. "You know, I think I can really relate to single parents. I mean—parents that have lost their spouses in death or through divorce. I feel this is sort of a test for me. It's a great responsibility raising kids alone."

"I'm sure it is," Anne agreed.

"Speaking of responsibility," chuckled Greg, "I think I owe a responsibility to myself to get out of the house one of these nights. Georgie ought to be feeling better by Friday, hopefully. I could get a baby-sitter and we could go out for dinner. Would you like to do that?"

"That sounds good."

"Great—I'll pick you up around seven-thirty?"

"Fine." Anne stood to leave. "Good-bye Georgie," Anne called toward his bedroom.

"Good-bye," Georgie yelled back. "Thanks for the stuff ya gots me!"

"You're welcome!" Anne reached for the doorknob. "Greg, have you heard anything from New York?"

"No. But if they offer me the job, I've decided I'll go."

Anne looked as if she had to force a smile. "Oh—that's great. But what about Georgie; is there any news on that?"

"Not really. I've got to get moving on that if anything is going to happen. They never call me. I understand they're really understaffed. I'll have to call them again."

"Well, I've got to get going. See you Friday then?" Anne opened the door.

"Yes, about seven-thirty. Bye, and thanks for getting the things for Georgie."

By night, Georgie had developed spots all over his body. Sleep was unheard of. Georgie had a high fever and was itching, even though Greg had given him a baking soda bath a half hour earlier. Finally, about four a.m., Georgie was sound asleep. Greg immediately went to bed.

Georgie woke up at eight a.m. Groggy and feeling rather dull, Greg heard Georgie walking to the bathroom and got up to check his spots. They were still red and itching, but his fever had broken. He was feeling much perkier.

Greg made Georgie a poached egg over toast and orange juice. Soon Georgie was up and about, watching TV and coloring. For the first time in two days Greg sat down at his drafting table.

After lunch, Greg decided to put Georgie down for a nap and call Miss Huntley to find out if there was any progress.

"Hello, Miss Huntley? This is Greg Larwell."

"Oh, hi. I'm glad you called. There have been some new developments in the last few days. I've got some good news and some not-so-good news."

"What?" Greg asked anxiously, his heart beginning to beat faster.

"First, since you didn't file breaking and entering charges against Georgie's mother, she was released from jail. Now she's gone again; no one knows where she is. She probably went back to West Virginia—or who knows! So the child welfare team took action a few days ago and recommended to the court that Georgie's mother be declared an unfit parent and that Georgie be declared adoptive."

"Was he?" Greg interrupted.

"Yes. The hearing was yesterday and the judge ruled Georgie be made an adoptive child."

"Super!" Greg yelled, then quickly remembered Georgie was taking a nap. Greg felt somewhat irritated at the welfare department for not keeping him informed. "I wish I would have known all this was happening—it would have eased my anxiety some."

"Yes, I'm sorry," Miss Huntley apologized. "We have been so overloaded here. Tell you what—you are still interested in adopting, aren't you?"

"Yes," Greg answered quickly. That "yes" was one of the most important words he had said in his life. Not only had Georgie psychologically and emotionally affected his present life, but would affect the rest of his life!

"Then I'd like to do another home study," Miss Huntley said excitedly. "I realize you've already had home studies for foster parenting, but adoptive studies are also required by law. When would it be convenient for you? The sooner the better."

"Right now Georgie has the chicken pox. How about the first full week in June? School will be out then."

"Okay—let me look at my date book . . . how is June

sixth? That's a Monday.''

"Fine. What time?''

"Does noon suit you?''

"Yes, that's fine.''

"Okay, Greg. Oh, and maybe you shouldn't tell Georgie right now about his mother's hearing or about his being adoptive. Tell him eventually, but just play it by ear—whenever the time is right.''

"By the way—I almost hate to ask you, but what was the not-so-good news?''

"Yes,'' Miss Huntley acknowledged. "The Circuit Court judge is tough. He has some very antiquated ideas about adoptions. I was just concerned, as you were, that being single might affect his decision. Judges have a great amount of power. It's scary sometimes how much power they really have. Well, anyway, we'll cross that bridge when we come to it. You just let us work on that. Don't worry, we'll present him a good case.''

"But what if he would deny adoption?''

"Then we would appeal and go to a higher court—in this case, Superior Court. There would be a different judge involved.''

"Thanks so much, Miss Huntley. I'm really enthused about this. You **will** keep me informed regularly, won't you?''

"Yes, I promise. As soon as all the preliminaries are taken care of, the case ought to go fast. See, because there are no relatives interested in Georgie and no known father, things will probably go fast. As I had mentioned to you another time, kids in Georgie's position, who are out of infancy, are hard to place. So when there is a good adoptive home, things move fast.''

"Okay.'' Greg gave a relieved sigh. "Thanks again. Good-bye.''

The next night Greg thought Georgie was feeling almost back to normal. His spots had signs of beginning scabs and he thought there would be no problem leaving Georgie for the evening.

Theo readily accepted a call to baby-sit. It was Theo's weekend to have Karen and she had had the chicken pox a year ago. When Theo and Karen arrived, Theo kidded Greg. "Now listen, Greg. You know how I worry. You must be in by eleven o'clock!" Greg and Theo laughed.

"By the way, Theo, I've been thinking seriously about what we were talking about in Indianapolis." Greg looked around to make sure Georgie and Karen couldn't hear him. They were busily playing with some old model cars he had assembled as a young boy. "You know, about adoption. In fact, things might be moving fast very soon."

Theo slapped Greg on the back. "Hey, I'm really excited and proud for you. That's neat."

"Thanks, Theo. And you know, I might ask you for some legal advice somewhere along the line if I run into a snag. I realize you're a corporate lawyer—but I suppose you could help some," Greg joked.

Greg and Anne went out of town to a little country restaurant. The restaurant had a relaxing atmosphere. A pianist played soft, soothing music.

It was an evening of mutual enjoyment. They each shared different experiences and feelings, freely and naturally. Greg could not imagine moving to New York and never seeing Anne again. Not now. There was something special about their relationship. Their being together had confirmed his feelings. What if marriage were in the future? There always seemed to be a barrier where New York was concerned. But one thing he knew . . . that he loved Anne.

Chapter 16

The last day of school was a joyous occasion for Georgie. He had finished all the school work he missed when he had the chicken pox. Now he was going to be home all day, every day.

Greg decided to go on a stricter work schedule, working more when Georgie was sleeping and spending more time with him during the day.

Georgie had signed up for the summer baseball program sponsored by the community and school. The Junior Little League met five days a week, Monday through Friday from 10:00 a.m. to 1:00 p.m. Greg thought even though it would mean driving Georgie to and from school, it would provide him excellent working time while Georgie was at practice, and of course would be good for Georgie.

Monday morning, Greg drove Georgie to his first baseball practice. Georgie took along an old baseball mitt that Greg had used as a youngster.

As they drove up to the baseball diamond, Greg saw a woman dressed in a baseball uniform and cap standing on the pitcher's mound. She appeared to be giving directions and orders to the children. Getting out of his car, Greg looked closer at the woman. It was Anne!

He and Georgie walked up to Anne. Greg could not quite believe Anne was coaching. But sure enough, she had a patch on her uniform which said "Coach." She was holding a clipboard containing all the names of the children who had pre-registered for the program.

Greg did not doubt Anne's ability to run the summer program and coach; she was a very confident and strong-minded person. But it struck him as odd that such a re-fined, soft-spoken, and feminine individual would enjoy that kind of work.

"Hi, Coach," Greg said kiddingly and leaned around Georgie to whisper in her ear. "They didn't have coaches like you when I was in Little League. May I sign up?"

Anne smiled and then frowned at Greg. "Sorry, you're too late," she laughed. "Sign-up was last week."

"Well, good luck. I have to get to work. I sure don't envy you having sixty 'little ones' under your care."

"I really don't mind. In fact, it's fun. This is the second summer I've done it."

Greg laughed. "A glutton for punishment!"

"Hey," Anne giggled, "why don't you stay and be the assistant manager?"

Greg threw up his arms. "No thanks. Maybe next year," he laughed.

Georgie found his name on the list and Anne checked it. Then he spotted Henry and ran over to play catch.

"Well—home to work. Oh, by the way. This is the day Janet Huntley comes over to do the home study. Wish me luck."

"You don't need any luck, Greg. There's nothing to worry about. She knows you're a fit parent. You've proven that."

Greg left for home. He knew he had nothing to worry about as far as the home study. Yet, he could not help feeling a little apprehensive. It was such a big step.

At noon, Janet Huntley drove up in a little red Ford. Since it was a beautiful, warm summer day, they sat on lawn chairs on the grass.

"As I mentioned before, Greg, this home study is required by law. It's actually just a formality. But I might tell you that I—we, the child welfare team—think you are doing a great job with Georgie. He certainly has responded well to you."

"Yes, really, there haven't been any real problems to speak of."

"Let me ask you then a standard but necessary question." Miss Huntley got a pencil and pad from her brief case and leaned back in the lawn chair. "Why do you want to adopt a child—generally speaking?"

"That might be a standard question, but it's a tough one to pinpoint. Well, first of all, let me say that I didn't start out this whole thing with adoption in mind. In fact, it never entered my mind. I've really grown to love Georgie, and being a foster parent, I believe, is a two-way street. I think most foster parents need the children as much as the children need them. At least—it's that way between Georgie and me." Greg paused and rubbed his forehead. "Let me put it this way. I don't have children, but if I did, not adopting Georgie would be like giving up my own son."

"Georgie is an ideal child. Many foster children are angry, much more than Georgie. I'd say ninety percent of foster children have severe emotional or physical problems, or are destructive to property or steal."

"And he's very bright too," Greg interrupted. "His school grades are very good and he isn't too far behind grade level."

"I'd say that was remarkable. Georgie's an exceptional story. Most foster children have been bounced around the country so much and have so many problems that school really comes hard for them, understandably so."

"I thought Georgie would have had more academic problems with his mother's hassling and all. But he does great!" Greg boasted.

"That's good—I'm delighted! Next question. What about financial security? Do you think you would be able to handle the added expense of a child?" Miss Huntley smiled, "Our support checks stop once you adopt."

"That isn't anything great," Greg chuckled. "Seriously though, I see no problem. Two live as cheaply as one, as they say."

Miss Huntley asked several more questions and then got up to leave. "I guess that's all I need at this point. Oh, except, just for formality's sake, I need to go through the rooms of your house."

"I cleaned up just for you," Greg laughed. Miss Huntley quickly went through all the rooms.

"What happens now?" Greg asked.

"You wait again. We evaluate your home study and foster parenting; then we write up the report and present it to the judge, who in turn sets a hearing date. Fair enough?"

"If I can wait that long," Greg smiled.

That afternoon Greg went to pick up Georgie from baseball practice. Georgie and Anne were standing together at the front driveway of the school when he arrived. Georgie looked as if he had been crying.

"What's up?" Greg asked as he got out of the car.

"We had a little problem this afternoon. Georgie thought it was his turn to bat and he shoved another guy in line." Georgie looked up at Greg sheepishly. "The other guy thought it was his turn and shoved back," continued Anne. "Then they started slugging one another and it ended up a fist fight."

"Georgie!" Greg began. "You don't get anywhere by fighting. Sorry, Anne. I think Georgie and I will talk about this more seriously at home." Greg took Georgie's hand and led him to the car.

Georgie did not say a word all the way home. Greg could tell he was angry and pouting. When they got home, Greg sat Georgie on a kitchen chair to talk.

"Georgie, what do you think I ought to do? You know, you can't get mad at people like that and just **hit** them. That's not right. You should try to talk things out nicely."

"But he shoved me, too!" Georgie whined.

"Okay. But, from what I understand, you started the whole thing, right?"

"Ye-ah," Georgie cried.

"You should have asked—not shoved . . . don't you think?"

"I did ask! But he argued with me. It was my turn!"

Greg shuddered as he thought of having to spank Georgie. He had never done that. But in this case—? Greg took a deep breath. "Georgie. I think I'm going to have to spank you."

Georgie started a deep wailing which made Greg feel worse about spanking. But he knew he should not back down. Not now.

Greg leaned Georgie over his knee and gave him one "meaningful" whack. Georgie cried more. Greg thought for a moment he would cry, too! The old saying that "it hurts me worse than it hurts you" was true.

In a short time they were laughing and talking as usual. Georgie said he was sorry and then told Greg about his first day of Junior Little League. Henry was on Georgie's team, which seemed to make things more exciting for him.

"Hey, Daddy. Ya know—all the kids have bikes at Junior Little League, and they ride them there, too. I wish I had a bike," Georgie hinted rather broadly.

"I told you we'd see, Georgie. I'll really try to get you one this summer, okay?" Greg had already made up his mind to get Georgie a bicycle for his birthday. He would have to wait almost another month.

That evening after nine o'clock, Anne came over with some mint tea she had made. Georgie was already in bed, so Greg and Anne enjoyed the fresh drink on the front steps. The sun was setting, casting rays of orange, yellow, and red in the sky.

Greg sat their empty glasses on the ground and looked toward Anne. "I never have thanked you for showing such an interest in Georgie. He has really benefited from having you as a teacher and friend."

"It's hard not to take an interest in Georgie. He's a very likeable boy."

Greg reached over and held Anne's hand. "Anne . . . I'm glad I know you. You're really important to me. I . . . I guess I don't know how to tell you, but I feel a great deal for you."

"Thanks, Greg. You mean a lot to me, too, but—" Anne turned her head slightly.

Greg's heart took a leap, waiting for Anne to say she did not need him. "But what?"

"Well—I just don't know if I can get any more involved—knowing that you're thinking of moving to New York. That's so far away. I've prayed that I wouldn't be selfish, but it's really hard."

"I've thought the same thing, Anne. But earlier, I didn't know whether it mattered to you or not if I moved."

"Of course it did," Anne replied. "I didn't know how to tell you."

Greg sat up straight. "Well . . . I just won't take the job if it's offered to me," he said seriously. "I just won't take it."

"No, Greg. It's important to you. I've heard you say it and I can see it on your face. I don't want you not taking it because of me. Architecture is your life—think of the experience and opportunity."

"But you're a part of my life, too—a very important part. I don't want to be away from you."

There was silence for the next few minutes. It was getting humid, and the mosquitoes were starting to bite. Anne indicated it was getting late, and she left for her apartment.

Greg had a hollow feeling in his stomach, like nothing had been accomplished between Anne and him. Things seemed more complicated now.

"Dear Lord. Am I being selfish for wanting to go to New York? Am I using New York as an out? Or is it that I'm afraid to get involved because of what happened to Trudi? Lord, I **am** afraid of rejection; I know that. And I'm afraid of being left alone again. Please take the trauma of Trudi's memories from me, so that I may forgive that drunken driver and not be afraid to truly let myself go in faith, and express my love to Anne."

Chapter 17

The next Sunday morning after church, Greg and Georgie arrived home to find Janet Huntley at the front door. She waved to them as they got out of the car. Her face showed signs of stress and soberness, not at all like her usual business manner.

Greg wondered what she was doing here on a Sunday. Something about Georgie's adoption? Maybe the child welfare team did not accept the home study! Why would she make a special trip . . . on a Sunday?

"Hi, what's up?" Greg asked speculatively.

"Could I talk with you—alone—for a few minutes?" She glanced at Georgie and smiled.

"Yes, sure. Georgie? Change your clothes please, and play with your football for awhile. I want to talk with Miss Huntley."

"I'm hungry. When are we goin' ta eat?"

"Soon, Georgie. Just play for awhile, okay?"

"Okay," Georgie complied. He ran inside to change while Greg poured lemonade for Miss Huntley. Miss

Huntley sat in the living room. Georgie quickly changed and ran outside to play.

Greg handed Miss Huntley a glass of lemonade. "Is there anything wrong, Miss Huntley? You looked troubled."

"Yes, I'm afraid there is." Greg sat across from Miss Huntley. He had not the slightest idea what could be wrong. Yet, judging from her appearance, he didn't want to know.

"Georgie's mother—" Miss Huntley began, "was killed in an automobile accident last night."

"Oh, no!" Greg gasped.

"I was just informed about it an hour ago. I called my supervisor right away, and then she told me to get in touch with you."

"Oh, no," Greg repeated. "What are we going to do?" Suddenly, Greg felt a heavy, sickening pressure on his shoulders. He would have to tell Georgie!

"Where—how did it happen?"

"In Wheeling, West Virginia. His mother was intoxicated. She was driving at a high rate of speed and crossed the center line. The occupant of the other car was killed also."

A sudden rage engulfed Greg. Hadn't he prayed about forgiving Trudi's killer? Now, Georgie's mother! Killing an innocent person because of drunkenness! Think of the victim's family . . . what they all must be going through and what they will go through the rest of their lives!

"Oh, poor Georgie," Greg sighed, weakened by the news. "He's gone through so much already. And now this."

Miss Huntley cleared her throat. "We'll need to talk about getting Georgie to the funeral. It will be on Tuesday in Wheeling. There are two different ways of going about it. The welfare department will fly Georgie out; or, if you want, you could take him."

"Oh—I'll take him," Greg responded immediately.

"Either way, the department will pay for Georgie's jet fare. You know—it might be uncomfortable for you with the relatives around." Miss Huntley raised her hands in frustration. "I don't know! This is the first time anything like this has ever happened in one of my case loads." She sat back in the chair. "The adoption hearing date has been set for June twenty-fourth, on a Thursday. Let's see— that's about a week and a half from now. All I'm trying to say, I guess, is that cases like this are funny. The relatives don't want anything to do with a kid, until something like this happens. You don't have to worry about legalities; you're okay that way. But it could get sort of touchy, depending. I really have no idea! I'm just speculating."

"You mean they could try to take him away?"

"Possibly."

"Can they do that?"

"No. Not legally. Georgie is a ward of the court in Indiana. And the West Virginia officials had contacted immediate relatives of Georgie's at our request, inquiring if there were any interested parties on Georgie's behalf. Not one person responded. So everything is 'go' for you, June twenty-fourth."

Just then Georgie came bursting into the house. "I'm hungry, Daddy," he said whining. "Ain't we goin' ta eat?"

Greg was speechless. It was hard for him to react normally to Georgie. How was he going to tell him? "In a little bit," Greg said softly, trying to speak in spite of a large, thickened lump in his throat.

"Would you like me to stay awhile, Greg?" Miss Huntley asked, implying she would stay and help tell Georgie.

"No—that's okay, I'll be alright."

"What'll be all right?" Georgie cut in.

"Never mind," Greg smiled and turned back to Miss

Huntley. "Thanks for coming over."

After Miss Huntley left, Greg made Georgie lunch. He tried to maintain a normal atmosphere. He needed time to think. Telling Georgie his mother was dead might be the hardest thing he would ever have to do. Georgie's knowing that his mother did not want him made it an even more delicate situation than under ordinary circumstances.

At least now it would not be necessary to tell Georgie that his mother could never have him back, that she was proven unfit, and that he had been deemed an adoptive child. Emotionally, it would be better for Georgie to think he was adoptive because his mother was dead.

Georgie lay on the floor and started laughing at an old comedy rerun on TV. He giggled and rolled over, pounding his fist on the floor. He seemed so happy. How could he break the news to him?

Several times that afternoon Greg attempted to tell Georgie about his mother. Each time Greg felt too much anxiety to go through with it. Now it was getting too late in the evening. He could not tell Georgie before bedtime. But he needed to be told soon!

The nightmarish day brought unrest for Greg. He lay in bed not being able to sort out, or come to a reasonable conclusion, as to what to say to Georgie. However, in the morning Georgie would have to be told, and they would fly to Wheeling in the afternoon.

Greg served Georgie cereal and juice for breakfast. Greg was tired and too preoccupied to make a big breakfast. For that matter, he was too preoccupied to do any planning or thinking.

Georgie got dressed and went outside to play. Three times after breakfast Greg had attempted to tell Georgie. How could he start the conversation? Greg's concentration was broken by the telephone ringing.

"Hello."

"Greg—I just heard about Georgie's mother. Why didn't you call me?" It was Anne. She sounded concerned, yet puzzled.

"I'm sorry. I've been in sort of a daze. How did you find out?"

"I ran into Janet Huntley downtown this morning. She told me. Can you talk right now?"

"Yes, Georgie's outside."

"What was Georgie's reaction?"

"I haven't told him yet. I don't know what to do! It's so hard. It's terrible, but I almost feel as sorry for myself for having to tell him as I do for him!"

"I'd be happy to be with you when you tell him—for moral support."

"Yes, please. I really need that. What about baseball practice?"

"No problem. I'll get someone to fill in for me today. I'll be right over."

Georgie came bounding into the house. "What time is it?" Georgie turned Greg's wrist to look at his watch even though he could not read the time.

"Almost ten," Greg answered.

"Hey, we're goin' ta be late for baseball practice. It starts at ten, don't it?"

"We're not going this morning, Georgie."

"Why?" Georgie moaned. Finally! Georgie had made an opening for him to begin the dreaded news.

"Because Georgie . . . something else came up. I'll tell you in a little bit." Greg paused. Give strength, Lord! Again he felt at a loss for the right words. Greg got the *Uno* cards and played a couple of games with Georgie to pass the time until Anne arrived.

A knock at the door made Greg jump. It was Anne. What had seemed like hours to Greg since she called had been only fifteen minutes. She let herself in. Her face was calm looking, her smile once again reassuring. Greg knew immediately that he could tell Georgie.

Anne sat down on the couch beside Greg. "I was just telling Georgie why we weren't going to baseball practice . . . We have to talk to you about something, Georgie."

"What?" Georgie grinned and shrugged his shoulders, amused at all the intense attention. He began throwing his football towards the ceiling and catching it.

"Come here, Georgie," Greg requested, extending Georgie his hand. "Sit down."

Georgie sat down between Greg and Anne. "Georgie," began Greg, "I've got something to tell you that's going to be hard for you to understand." Anne reached in front of Georgie and clasped Greg's hand. Georgie glanced at Anne, then Greg, seeming to realize the seriousness in Greg's voice.

"Am I bein' kicked off the baseball team or somethin'?" Georgie frowned.

"No, Georgie." Greg forced a smile. "It's nothing like that. It's about . . . about your mother." With his other hand Greg held Georgie's hand tightly. "She was in an accident, and she . . . she died, Georgie."

Georgie broke away from Greg and threw his football into the kitchen, hitting the table and chairs. "You're lying!" Georgie cried. "You're lying ta me!" Georgie ran from the room screaming and kicking everything in his path. He ran into his bedroom and slammed the door.

Instantly Greg got up to follow him into the bedroom. "No, Greg." Anne grabbed for Greg's arm. "Leave him alone right now. It's probably the best thing."

Greg sat down and deliberately nodded his head in agreement. "I guess you're right. I just feel so helpless, like a louse—like Georgie thinks it's my fault. What can I do?"

"Why don't we ask God for help and strength?" Greg and Anne sat back on the couch in silence. Anne's soothing manner put Greg at ease.

Several minutes went by before Georgie meekly came from his bedroom and walked toward Greg. His face was puffy from crying. Greg watched Georgie as he came to him. What a shame, thought Greg, that the last time Georgie saw his mother she was drunk and mean. But he must have seen her that way many times. Undoubtedly, it had not been a new experience.

Georgie reached out his arms for Greg. "I'm sorry, Georgie, I'm really sorry," Greg whispered.

Georgie looked directly at Greg. "Is Mommy with God— up there in heaven?" Georgie pointed upward.

"She's in His hands now," Greg answered.

"Is the good Holy Spirit goin' ta make her a good spirit, too?" Georgie whined.

"She's in God's hands, Georgie. He'll take care of her."

Greg held Georgie tightly. God and His mercy, thought Greg. He takes care of people, people with sick and twisted minds, like Georgie's mother.

Chapter 18

While Greg packed for the trip, Anne made airplane reservations to Wheeling. Two hours later, Greg and Georgie were on their way in a small private, twin engine aircraft.

They arrived in Wheeling in mid-afternoon. The rain poured without relief. After asking an airport attendant for the motel closest to the funeral home, Greg hired a taxi to take them there.

Georgie watched TV in their room while Greg used the lobby telephone to call the funeral home to see what arrangements had been made. He thought it best for Georgie not to hear his conversation with the funeral director.

"Good afternoon. Morgan Funeral Home. May I help you?"

"Yes. My name is Greg Larwell. Do you have the Stainer funeral tomorrow?"

"Yes, we do. It will be here at the funeral home at eleven a.m."

"Well, I'm a foster parent to the Stainer woman's son. We just flew in from Indiana."

"Then you'll want to come to the viewing this evening from seven 'til nine."

"No, I don't think so. It's been hard enough for Georgie, her son, without coming to that tonight."

"Yes, I'm sure it has. One thing I should mention is that the casket will be closed. She was in pretty bad shape from the accident. Since you're not coming tonight, I just thought I'd better say something to you, you know, so you can explain to her son ahead of time."

"Yes, I'm glad to know that. And one more thing. What about the other person who was killed?"

"Oh, yes. Very sad. We don't have his funeral, but it was a seventeen-year-old boy, just graduated from high school less than two weeks ago. He was going home from work. I guess it was a summer job he had taken. I understand he was a very bright boy and was planning to go into a pre-med program in college this fall."

Greg heard himself thank the funeral director for the information, but he began thinking about Trudi's funeral and her casket having to be closed. The young boy's family must be going through torment and hatred for Georgie's mother, as he had for the drunken driver that killed Trudi.

Georgie was lying on the bed crying when Greg got back to the room. Greg held him for several minutes. He was sorry he had left Georgie alone. He was too insecure right now. In fact, sitting around a motel room all evening seemed too grim under the circumstances.

The rain had stopped and the evening sun peeked through grayish clouds, promising a couple more hours of daylight. Greg and Georgie walked across the street to buy a hamburger at a McDonald's restaurant. While crossing, Greg noticed a park about a block from their motel.

After eating, Greg suggested to Georgie that they go for a walk and check out the park. But he only nodded and shrugged his shoulders.

It turned out to be a very nice park with footbridges, trails, playground equipment, and a little stream complete with beautiful lily pads and croaking frogs. As they walked along the stream, one minute Georgie would be talking non-stop, and the next minute he would be staring. The trip to the park ended with Greg pushing a silent Georgie on a long-chained swing.

At Georgie's bedtime, Greg turned on the air conditioner. Since the rain, the air had become muggy and humid.

Georgie lay his head back on the pillow and Greg covered him with the sheet. "What kind of accident was Mommy in?" Georgie looked at Greg with wide, wondering eyes. That was the first he had asked any questions about the accident.

Greg patted him on the shoulder. "It was a car accident, Georgie."

"Did it hurt her . . . I mean to die?" Georgie bit his lower lip.

Greg paused. Such hard questions about death no one had ever asked him. "Car accidents happen so fast . . . she probably never knew what happened. No, Georgie, it probably didn't hurt her." Greg hugged Georgie goodnight, hoping he had made him feel at least a little better by his answers and also hoping he would not ask any more questions about his mother. What more could he answer for him? It was so horrible and confusing for a child, especially an unloved child.

"Daddy?"

"What, Georgie?"

"Am I going to live with you . . . I mean, forever?"

It didn't seem an appropriate time to talk about adoption, yet Georgie needed that security, to belong. Maybe he could handle the funeral better having the assurance he would not be abandoned.

"Would you like to live with me?"

"Uh-huh, I like it with you," he smiled. Suddenly Georgie sat up in bed and, with a gleam in his eye, said, "How come you ain't married?" The question was asked in the spunky way that Georgie usually asked a question.

"No one's ever asked me to marry them," Greg laughed.

"No, really!" Georgie said, slightly aggravated.

"Why? Do you think I should be?"

"Yeah," Georgie answered shyly.

"Well, maybe someday I will get married," Greg smiled.

Georgie lay back down. Greg wondered how far he should continue the conversation about adoption, but decided to continue cautiously. "Georgie, do you know what the word 'adopt' means?"

"Yeah . . . I think so."

"Can you tell me what it means?"

"It means that some people get kids who don't have no place ta go and keep 'em."

"That's right. Would you like for me to adopt you? Then we would be a real family. You wouldn't be a foster son anymore, and I wouldn't be a foster daddy. We would be a **real** daddy and son."

Georgie didn't say anything, but he didn't need to. He grinned ear to ear, his face radiant. That was what Georgie wanted and needed to hear—the assurance that someone loved him, someone cared, that he had a home and family. Without further conversation, Georgie hugged Greg and then soon fell asleep.

The next morning Greg explained to Georgie that the casket would be closed. Georgie asked no questions. Judging from Georgie's reaction, Greg doubted he had ever been to a funeral.

Greg was more than curious about Georgie's relationship with his relatives. He could not imagine that none of them wanted Georgie. "Georgie, do you know any of your relatives?"

"My what?"

"Your relatives—like a grandfather, grandmother, aunt, uncle, and cousins."

"Oh yeah. I know my grandpa and grandma—kind of."

"When did you see them last?"

"I dunno. But I remember one time bein' at their house and they was shellin' peas—and every once in a while my grandpa would tell me ta open my mouth, and he'd pop a pea in there. I like raw peas." Georgie opened his mouth and pointed inside.

"Do you remember being with them other times?"

"Yeah, one other time. They came up to Wheeling ta visit us."

"Where did they live?" Greg interrupted.

"They was from Boggs."

"Boggs?"

"Yeah, Boggs, West Virginia. Anyways—when they come up they argued a lot with Mommy. I could hear them when I was supposed ta be sleepin' in my room."

"What did they argue about, Georgie?"

"I don't remember."

"Are there any other relatives you know?"

"Yeah—Aunt Betty. But her and Mommy argued a lot too."

"What did they argue about?"

"Aunt Betty used ta say that Mommy and I didn't love Jesus because we didn't go ta church. But Mommy said that we didn't hav-ta go ta church because we watched that guy on TV."

At the funeral home they were greeted warmly at the inside entrance by the director. Greg began to feel weak from anticipation. How would Georgie's relatives react to him, to Georgie?

Upon entering the service room, Greg saw about twenty people sitting in the front two rows of seats facing the casket. He glanced up and down the rows, amazed at how well-dressed everyone was. He had expected these hill people to look like the stereotypes portrayed in films and on TV.

Two baskets of flowers were on either side of the casket. Recorded organ music came through speakers in the ceiling. A large man in a black, ill-fitted suit and carrying a Bible followed Greg and Georgie through the doorway.

"Good morning, brothers," the man smiled sincerely and extended his hand to Greg. "Are you the bereaved family?"

Greg shook his hand, surmising he was the minister in charge. "Well, eh . . . this is the son, Georgie. I'm Greg Larwell, Georgie's foster father."

"Oh, yes," the man said, squeezing Georgie's hand, "I'm terribly sorry, Georgie." He shook Greg's hand and then proceeded to the front of the room. Georgie seemed to be in a daze, staring aimlessly around the room.

The people who were already seated realized Greg and Georgie were standing in the back. They looked around whispering to one another.

Greg and Georgie started for a seat, but before they could get to one an attractive woman in her early forties came up to them.

"Hello, Georgie," she said coldly and without smiling. "Do you remember me?" Georgie meekly nodded his head acknowledging her presence.

"Yeah, you're Aunt Betty," Georgie said without expression, seeming to sense the cold tone in his aunt's voice.

"And you must be Georgie's foster parent, Mr.—?"

"Larwell, Greg Larwell. Nice to meet you."

"Yes, well all I can say is you must be a saint. Marge, Georgie's mother, could never seem to handle him."

Greg quickly looked at Georgie, not quite believing she would say that kind of thing in front of the child. He put his arm around Georgie's shoulders. "Oh, we get along just fine—he's a very good boy."

Just then the funeral director walked up to them and indicated it was time for the service to begin. The minister prayed aloud and then began to preach. Greg could not concentrate on listening, thinking about the rudeness Georgie's aunt had displayed. Poor Georgie. She made it sound as if he were to blame for his mother's problems. As Greg was thinking, some familiar words the minister was reciting caught his attention.

"I will lift up my eyes to the hills, from whence does my help come? My help comes from the Lord, who made heaven and earth."

The words were comforting, especially because of the circumstances. Someday, thought Greg, he would teach Georgie those words and explain to him the comfort to be received from them.

After the service, Greg quickly took Georgie past the people to one of the baskets of flowers. He wanted Georgie to pick a flower to place on the casket and instructed him to do so. Then the two of them stood in front of the casket in silence for a few moments. Georgie placed the flower on the top of the casket and stepped back one step. Without any warning, he started to cry as if he suddenly realized his mother was inside that huge, gray, metal box. Georgie then slid to the floor and continued the tearful outburst. "I want my Mommy," Georgie sobbed over and over.

Greg knelt and held Georgie's head to him while he sobbed for several minutes with great heaves of sadness. Everyone else in the room remained seated, some crying because of Georgie's emotional display and some staring without expression at the casket.

When Georgie's crying subsided, Greg whispered in his ear, "Georgie, your mommy . . ." Greg stopped, trying to keep his own composure. He swallowed hard and bit tightly on his lip. "Your mommy loved you very, very much. Never forget that. Sometimes she had trouble showing how much she loved you because she had a few problems. You'll remember that she loved you— won't you, Georgie?"

Georgie bravely rubbed his eyes and then looked at Greg. "I'll remember." Greg hugged Georgie and they stood up. Their moment of solitude was interrupted by Georgie's aunt and an elderly man and woman walking up to them.

"This is your grandpa and grandma," blurted Georgie's aunt. "Don't you know them, boy? You should greet them properly with respect."

"Lay off the boy," the man said sternly, and then turned toward Georgie. "How are ya, Georgie? We haven't saw you in a long time. You've grown just like a weed." The grandfather touched Georgie's shoulders and then the grandmother gently hugged him to her.

"Little Georgie—how we wish we could see you more often." Georgie blushed and looked at the floor. The grandmother seemed kind, but she appeared weak and in poor health, with her stooped posture reflecting the burdens of her life.

"Where are you people from?" Greg said, attempting to make conversation to ease the situation. He was taken by surprise to find Georgie's grandparents to be gracious and respectable people.

"We're from Boggs—that's about eighty-five miles due east of Charleston. Boggs is in Webster County."

The directions and locations meant absolutely nothing to Greg, but he smiled and acknowledged the grandfather, trying to appear interested to lighten the uncomfortable meeting.

Greg was becoming more and more interested in Georgie's family situation. They didn't seem close to each other nor did they seem to know their grandson and nephew very well. Greg decided he needed to know some answers to his questions.

"Could I talk to you people alone for a few minutes?" Greg felt bold to be asking—yet he couldn't go back to Indiana without clearing up some important issues he had on his mind. The kindly minister heard Greg ask to talk to Georgie's family and offered to take Georgie outside. Meanwhile, the pallbearers were moving the casket out of the service room. The four adults walked to the lobby and were seated on two large Victorian couches.

"I don't want to appear nosy," Greg began, "but I'm confused at some things and then there are some things I think you should know . . ." Greg felt awkward as the three people waited for his next comments. Greg looked at Georgie's grandparents. "My name is Greg Larwell, by the way. I don't think we were introduced." The two men shook hands.

"Go on, Mr. Larwell," the grandfather gestured.

"Do you know that Georgie has been made adoptive by the court's action—and that I'm in the process of adopting him?"

"Yes," Georgie's aunt snapped. "And did you know that Georgie is a woods-rabbit?—you know—illegitimate."

"Betty!" the grandfather said sharply, raising his voice. "For once in your life, would ya please shut up!" Georgie's aunt sat back hard on the couch, folding her arms in disgust.

The grandfather turned to Greg, pausing a moment to regain his thoughts. "I know you must wonder what kind of family we are—not to take Georgie in. The welfare contacted us, but we had to say no."

"I'm sure you must have your reasons—" Greg was still trying to fit the pieces of the puzzle together.

"Marge, Georgie's mother, isn't really our daughter. You see, when she was an infant, we found her in a little basket on our doorstep, and we never knew where she came from. At the time, Betty was almost ten and we couldn't have any more children. We thought it was a blessing from the Lord. So we tried our level best to raise her as our own."

"And she's always been a problem," the aunt blurted cattily, "just as Georgie will be. It's in their blood, if you know what I mean—you just can't change 'em." She glanced at her father, and then quickly looked away.

"Well, there are several reasons why we can't take him, Mr. Larwell," the grandfather continued, obviously more upset with each interruption. "One, we have a very small pension—we barely get by on it. And two, we're too old. I'll be sixty-nine next month and Mom is sixty-eight. Neither of us is in good health. I think it would be too much for us to take on."

"And now **I'll** tell you **my** reasons for not taking him," Georgie's aunt said bitterly.

"That's not necessary," the grandfather cut in.

"You're right on that," she snapped. "I'm not going to explain myself to him," she pointed to Greg, "just explain a few things about Marge."

She turned and looked directly at Greg. It was hard for him to look her directly in the eye. She seemed so hateful.

"First of all, Mr. Larwell, Marge has always been a

burden to my folks. Why—they're old before their time because of that girl." She pointed to the casket as the pallbearers placed it inside the hearse. "She always liked the guys. To make a long story short—she did some hookin' here in Wheeling every time she was out of a job—which was most of the time. She drained Daddy and Mom of their money and spent it on booze and drugs. Well, Georgie's a product of her hookin'—and that's the truth. And after she had Georgie, she and Georgie stayed in Wheeling permanently—which was okay by me. Why—look at her life. She messed it up to her dying day—killing an innocent boy!"

"That's enough now, Betty," the grandfather scolded, raising himself up stiffly on the couch.

"No, there's just one more thing I want to say, and you can quote me to whoever you want to. I refused all along to have anything to do with her after she started making trips to Wheeling. I knew what she was up to. Georgie is a bastard—a disgrace to our name—and I refuse to take any responsibility in the situation!" She stood up abruptly and walked out of the room.

Greg felt embarrassed for himself and for Georgie's grandparents. The grandmother who had been crying silently, took Greg's hand. "We want you to take Georgie. It's the only chance he has in life. We just feel very sorrowful about the whole thing, but we will feel happier now, won't we?" She looked at her frail, graying husband.

"Yes, it's a real blessing to know that Georgie will be brought up right."

Greg squeezed the grandmother's hand. "You are two wonderful people," Greg said softly. "And you can bet that I'll include you both in Georgie's life. We'll try to visit once a year and Georgie will write to you."

"The Lord bless you," the grandfather whispered, and then everyone stood.

The minister brought Georgie in from the outside. "It's time to go to the cemetery now," he said quietly.

"Thank you," Greg said, extending his hand to the minister. "I don't think Georgie and I will go." Greg leaned over to the minister and whispered, "I think little Georgie has had a full enough day, wouldn't you say?" The minister nodded his head in agreement. Then Greg turned to Georgie.

"Georgie, you are going to be seeing much more of your grandparents from now on. They love their grandson and want to keep in touch with him."

Georgie spontaneously hugged his grandparents and they freely returned the gesture of love. Georgie had lost his biological mother, gained nonbiological and loving grandparents, and soon would legally gain a father for the first time in his life.

The plane ride home was rough. The little aircraft bumped constantly. It was raining and storming. Georgie sat stiffly in his seat, covering his eyes at every bolt and flash of lightning. The other eight passengers also showed signs of fright.

Georgie had not spoken one complete sentence since they left the funeral home. He seemed stunned at all the events connected with the funeral, and Greg sensed a distance between them.

As the storm worsened, there were now "oooh's" and "ah's" coming from the passengers.

A kindly old priest, sitting across the aisle from Greg and Georgie observed Georgie's rigidity and leaned over to talk to him. "Don't worry, son," he said thoughtfully, "we'll get out from under this storm soon." Georgie smiled nervously at him. "Would you like to play a guessing game?" the priest asked.

Georgie shyly nodded his head. He got up from his seat and joined the priest. Georgie was soon laughing and talking and had completely forgotten about the turbulence.

After the storm had died down considerably, the priest smiled at Greg as Georgie moved back to his seat. "There you go," he said. "I'll give you back to your dad again."

"Thanks," Georgie responded.

Chapter 19

Georgie played his first baseball game on Wednesday, a week after the funeral. The funeral had drained Georgie emotionally, and it was like pulling teeth for Greg to get him out of the house for baseball practices. Georgie would periodically go into deep depressions, sleeping more than usual. On the other hand he showed great dependency on Greg, wanting to please him by cleaning his room and watering the plants and flowers. Greg thought Georgie was very insecure and needed to do things to assure his love for him.

Anne had invited Greg and Georgie to her apartment to eat a few times that week to help take some pressure off Greg and to keep Georgie from dwelling on his mother. Greg and Anne's relationship was becoming more and more trustworthy, and it was increasingly hard for both to think about their being separated by the New York job offer.

During Georgie's game on Wednesday he hit a double, batting a run in. Greg yelled throughout the game to the point he felt a little ridiculous afterward. He felt like the stereotyped pushy parent at his kid's baseball game! Greg could see that the game helped Georgie's ego and that it was helping to build his self-confidence.

The game had also taken Greg's mind off the adoption hearing that was scheduled for the next morning at ten-thirty. With the funeral and trying to catch up on his drawings, he hadn't had much time to think about the hearing. He had decided it was too late to start worrying now and had left it in God's hands.

The next morning, Anne picked up Georgie so Greg could have the day free. As Greg climbed the courthouse steps, a positive feeling came over him. He had all the qualifications of a good parent! Most importantly, he loved the child and Georgie loved him. What more could the judge ask?

Janet Huntley was waiting for Greg at the courtroom door. "Hi, Greg," she smiled. "Are you ready?"

"Well, I'm beginning to get a little nervous, but I feel confident about the adoption."

"Good. So do I. Don't worry. And don't let Judge Johnston fluster you. He will ask you some questions, but Mr. James, the welfare department attorney, will handle most of it."

"Who will be here today?" Greg inquired.

"It will be an informal, closed hearing. All adoption hearings are closed with only the immediate people involved in attendance. Sometimes a psychiatrist or character witnesses are asked to appear. But, we didn't think it was necessary in this case. Your foster parent record will speak for itself. The only people here today will be Mr. James, Judge Johnston, a court recorder, and you and I."

"What'll I call him? 'Your Honor?' "

"No—'Judge' is used more in informal hearings." Miss

Huntley opened the door and they walked in. After brief introductions were made, the hearing began. Mr. James started by reading some of the legal background for Judge Johnston. Then Miss Huntley briefed the judge on particulars in Georgie's case history.

After Mr. James and Miss Huntley finished, the judge sat back in his large wooden chair and pensively bit on a pencil. Only a few seconds had gone by, but Greg thought it seemed like hours! Finally, the judge's eyes met Greg's, as if he were ready to ask him some questions. Greg felt uncomfortable, remembering how Miss Huntley had described this judge as being conservative.

"Mr. Larwell," the judge said authoritatively, "do you consider yourself to be a logical person—a person who thinks things through?"

What kind of question is that? thought Greg. What did that have to do with anything? He heard himself say, "Yes."

"How so?"

"Well . . . I'm a free-lance designer. I think that takes a great amount of self-discipline."

The judge chuckled condescendingly. "No, young man. I didn't ask you if you were self-disciplined; I asked you if you were logical. You **do** know the difference—don't you?"

"Yes," Greg laughed nervously.

"Okay, let me ask you in another way." The judge shifted his position in his chair. "Have you **logically** thought of the responsibility involved with an adoption? You **know**, foster parenting and adoption are two very different areas. If you have trouble with a foster child, all you have to do is call the welfare department and they'll move the child to another home. But if you're an adoptive parent . . . well, I want to be sure you're aware of the difference."

"Yes, sir," Greg said confidently. "I'm aware of the difference and I'm ready for it."

"Let me point out, Judge Johnston," Mr. James interrupted, "since the mother is now deceased and no other natural parent is established and there are no interested relatives, Georgie is adoptive."

"Yes, I know that, Mr. James," the judge snapped.

"Excuse me, Judge Johnston," Mr. James apologized. "But the point I was trying to make was why should the child stay in a series of foster homes until he is eighteen when Mr. Larwell is ready and willing to adopt?"

"Thank you, Mr. James," the judge said and turned to Greg. "Mr. Larwell—do you have any future marriage plans?" The judge leaned back and folded his hands on his chest.

Here it comes! thought Greg. This is what he had dreaded. "Well, sir . . . I—"

"Excuse me, Judge Johnston," Mr. James interrupted again. "I'm sure Your Honor is aware that the law does not require a two-parent fam—"

"Mr. James! I'm fully aware of that fact. I just asked Mr. Larwell a simple question. Now, I would appreciate it if you would let him answer—with no more interruptions!" Mr. James put Greg in mind of an ambitious young lawyer, fresh out of law school and anxious to reveal what knowledge he had acquired.

"Now, Mr. Larwell," continued Judge Johnston, "your ah . . . marriage plans?"

"I have no immediate plans, sir. However, someday I'd like to marry, yes."

"That's fine to say, but what about now? Based on my interpretation of the existing laws in the State of Indiana, it seems a two-parent situation is ideal. Wouldn't you say so, Mr. Larwell?"

Greg wanted to ask him his "interpretation of the existing laws," but felt it better just to answer the question and not push matters. "From what I understand, Judge Johnston, children past infancy are hard to place in adoptive homes. Georgie and I are comfortable together, and I want to adopt him. Don't you think that holds some merit?" Greg asked politely.

"And consider state and county taxes, Judge Johnston," Mr. James interjected. "Foster children are taxpayers' headaches." Greg thought it sounded like Mr. James was talking about a piece of meat—not a person!

"Yes, Mr. James," the judge answered, annoyed. "I'm also aware of the tax dollar, thank you." Judge Johnston cleared his throat. "Now, then, Mr. Larwell, back to your statement. Yes, that does hold merit. I just want you to be extremely cautious about what you're taking on, a sobering responsibility."

Greg leaned forward in his intensity and placed his elbows on the table.

"Sir, it's beyond responsibility . . . I love the boy. I think I have the qualifications and capabilities of a caring parent. I'm ready to rear him to the best of my ability—ethics, morals, values, a Christian atmosphere."

The judge frowned as if in deep concentration and mused, "Well, Mr. Larwell, you present a convincing argument." The judge pondered. He adjusted his glasses and slowly rubbed his nose. Greg literally held his breath; his arm muscle twitched. Please God, Greg thought to himself.

"Mr. Larwell . . ." The judge took off his glasses. "I cannot agree that single parenting is the best circumstance for a youngster to grow up in. Psychologically, it's been proven through studies, that children function best with a 'mother-father' environment. They need both to give them their identify." The judge shuffled some papers, appearing to be ready to adjourn. "My first inclination is to say no . . . but somehow, that doesn't seem to be fair in this case—to you **or** the boy. You seem to be an honest, straight-forward individual . . ." The judge put his glasses back on and folded his hands on the table. "Mr. Larwell—I am granting you the adoption on the basis of the circumstances as presented and of your good character." The judge stood up, with everyone present following his move. He smiled and extended his hand to Greg. "Good luck," he said to Greg as if he were sending him on an important mission. And to Greg, it was a mission.

After Judge Johnston left the courtroom, Greg joyfully hugged Miss Huntley and exuberantly shook Mr. James' hand. He couldn't wait to see Anne and Georgie. They would still be at baseball practice, so he would have to wait until one o'clock and then go to Anne's apartment. He could go to the baseball field, but he wanted to see them alone.

At twelve-thirty, Greg was surprised to see Anne and Georgie coming in the drive. Anne explained she had gotten a substitute to take over the baseball practice because she and Georgie could not take the suspense any longer.

"Well?" Anne asked apprehensively. Georgie stood beside Anne at the door holding her hand. Greg smiled as it reminded him of the first time he saw Georgie standing at the front door holding Miss Huntley's hand. And now he was his son!

"Yes!" laughed Greg. "Yes!" He picked Georgie up and swung him around. "You're officially my son now!"

"Ya mean you're my daddy now . . . for **real**?"

"You bet!" Greg shouted excitedly. Greg looked at Anne and saw she was crying. Greg went over to hug her and whispered in her ear, "I love you." He turned around and grabbed Georgie. The three of them laughed and cried together for several minutes with joyful laughter and tears. After Greg gave them a few details of the court hearing, he sat down on the living room chair, with Georgie and Anne sitting in front of him on the floor.

"There will be no New York for us, Georgie," Greg announced affectionately. Georgie looked at him strangely not knowing anything about the New York deal. Georgie's puzzlement turned into a smile. It didn't matter what Greg said. Anything his new father said was okay with Georgie. Then Greg's eyes met Anne's. Her eyes sparkled; she understood completely what "no New York" meant. "We're staying right here—this is our home."

The next week at Georgie's birthday party, Greg presented him with a brand new bicycle. Anne, Theo, Karen, Henry, and Miss Huntley were there—Georgie's best friends.

Greg leaned back and watched Georgie unwrap the other presents. Georgie was happy, contented. It was hard to believe that only a few short months ago his future was so uncertain. But now Georgie was his, legally and emotionally. "My little Georgie," whispered Greg.

DAVID WARREN SWARTLEY writes *My Little Georgie* out of his wealth of experience as a foster parent and a deep, caring concern for the homeless children of the world.  He has been the foster father of four boys, and has been involved in Big Brothers/Big Sisters, both as a Big Brother and as a board member. In addition, he has served as a child-care worker at Bashor Home, a residential home for children.

Mr. Swartley teaches fourth grade at Jefferson Elementary School in Goshen, Indiana, where he lives. He has also written *My Friend, My Brother,* published in 1980.